U0165721

ENGLISH GRAMMAR AND RHETORIC

陳錦芬 著

英語
文法 與 修辭

五南圖書出版公司 印行

作者序

　　本書是文法與修辭的合訂本，修辭事實上就是文法的內涵與衍生。修辭是在文法架構和元素之下，寫作者透過特殊的寫作技巧（修辭）的應用，凸顯其理念或信息的特殊性和其學術寫作的層級。也因為其特殊的寫作技巧，強烈吸引閱讀者的注意和興趣，進而深刻地印（imprint）在閱讀者的腦海裡。可知，修辭沒有文法無法作精闢的呈現，文法沒有修辭顯現不出其價值所在。簡言之，文法與修辭是一體，不可分的。因此，本書的架構不同於一般的文法用書，將文法概念和修辭技巧分開介紹。本書將這兩大層面整合為一。學習者除了必須具備整體的文法原則概念之外，還需要精熟修辭技巧，才能作深入的閱讀和寫出精湛洗練的文章。

　　本書雖然以英文基本句型架構、名詞（含代名詞）、動詞、語氣、形容詞與副詞、副詞子句、形容詞子句、名詞子句、介系詞、倒裝句等文法章節來組織，但特定的修辭特質都融合到各個相關章節裡。例如：傳統英文修辭書會從明喻（Similes）、隱喻（Metaphors）、矛盾詞（Oxymoron）、反襯法（Antimetathesis）、平行結構（Parallelism）、擬人法（Personification），到特殊句型，如分裂句（clef sentence）、where…there、倒裝句、雙重否定、雙重比較等類別來組織英文修辭書的章節。在本書中，明喻、隱喻和雙重比較整合在第十一章比較結構的章節介紹；平行結構的修辭技巧就在第七章合句中說明。Where…there 和雙重否定（not…until）屬於副詞子句的衍生句型，故整合到第八章副詞子句中詳述；倒裝句則另闢章節第十二章來詳解；至於 if 假設語氣中的省略句就是屬於修辭倒裝句的一種，爲了以全觀點的概念分類，則整放在第四章動詞 II 中的「語氣」來說明。此外，每個重要的修辭概念會配合實例來闡述之，如：

引用美國第一夫人希拉蕊的自傳 "A Chicago native, Mrs. Clinton grew up in suburban Park Ridge, Illinois as a close-knit family. Throughout her childhood, the foundations of her lasting commitment to family, work and service were established. It is this commitment and the belief that we 'all have an obligation to give something of ourselves to our community,' that has helped to shape her role as our nation's First Lady. " 其中的 It is …that 就是強而有力的名詞子句作爲同位語之用和分裂句（Cleft sentence）的整合，即是修辭中的特殊句型，在本書中就在「名詞子句」與「分裂句」的章節中詳述。

簡言之，修辭就是文法架構的衍生和技巧性的應用，唯整合到相關文法概念中解說和練習，才能充分掌握英文文法的完整性和精隨。

此外，本書最值得英文學習者擁有和詳讀的理由是整本書以淺顯的文字及全觀的觀點來解說「文法與修辭」的內涵，並提供大量「英文文法與修辭」相關例句和「實戰」考題，加上精闢詳盡的分析與解說，能充分協助英語文法初學者輕易掌握文法脈絡，更讓學習英文文法多年的讀者豁然了解他們曾經學過的英文是那麼有系統和合乎邏輯思考，不是他們一直害怕的英文文法。只要有清楚明確的文法知識和修辭技巧，即使是一篇充滿單字的文章和考題，仍能作充分的理解文章內涵和準確的解題。加油！

>>> **本書適用對象：**

英語文法的初學者、準備英語認證考試的考生（英文能力認證標準測驗、高普考、教師甄選、公私立機構語言檢測等）、教授文法的英文教師、英文翻譯工作者。

目 錄

>>> 作者序

>>> 第一章　句子基本結構　　　001

    Exercise 1　　　005

>>> 第二章　名詞　　　009

    Exercise 2　　　015

>>> 第三章　動詞 I　　　027

    Exercise 3　　　031

>>> 第四章　動詞 II　　　041

    Exercise 4　　　045

>>> 第五章　形容詞與副詞　　　053

    Exercise 5　　　056

>>> 第六章　There, It　　　065

    Exercise 6　　　068

>>> 第七章　合句　　　071

    Exercise 7　　　073

>>> 第八章　副詞子句　081

Exercise 8　086

>>> 第九章　形容詞子句　095

Exercise 9　098

>>> 第十章　名詞子句　107

Exercise 10　112

>>> 第十一章　比較結構　121

Exercise 11　126

>>> 第十二章　倒裝句　135

Exercise 12　139

>>> 第十三章　介系詞　143

Exercise 13　147

>>> 總複習　155

Review 1　156

Review 2　164

>>> 問題解答　173

第一章

# 句子基本結構
>>> EXERCISE 1

I、簡單句（Simple Sentence）：一個子句（clause）組成之句子（sentence）。

II、合句（Compound Sentence）：二個以上的子句組成之句子，成對稱結構。

III、複句（Complex Sentence）：二個以上的子句組成之句子，成附屬結構。

>>> I、簡單句（Simple Sentence）

簡單句乃由單一子句（一個主詞＋一個動詞）所組成之句子。

及物動詞	＋受詞	＋附加句
・主詞＋不及物動詞＋介系詞	＋受詞	
連綴動詞	＋補語（N、ADJ、ADV）	

例句：A major step in the development of algebra was the evolution
of an accurate understanding of negative quantities.

此句爲簡單句，主詞是一個名詞片語 a step，唯一的動詞是 was，受詞爲 the evolution。其餘的介系詞片語（介＋名詞片語）皆擔任形容詞或副詞的功能。of algebra(adj. ph.) 修飾 development（幾何的發展），in the development 修飾 step（發展的一大步）。所以，此句的主詞（A major step in the development of algebra）爲「幾何發展的一大步」。此句的受詞（the evolution of an accurate understanding of negative quantities）則爲「負量準確理解的演化」。可知簡單句的句子長度可以很長，甚至如同 A4 紙那麼長，如果只有一個動詞就視爲簡單句。

II、合句（Compound Sentence）

合句乃二個或二個以上的簡單句平行組合而成的對等子句。這二個句子在整個敘述句中的分量同等，藉助對等連接詞（but, or, and, yet）來銜接或組合。連接詞兩邊可能是對稱的兩個句子、兩個動詞片語、兩個名詞片語或介系詞片語。合句一般以平行結構的型態出現。

例句：Forests <u>provide natural beauty</u>, <u>prevent erosion</u> and <u>furnish food</u> for wildlife.

此句的主詞為 Forests，有三個動詞 provide, prevent, furnish，說明森林的三大功能，由一個對等連接詞 and 來銜接。這是三個句子的整合，功能、位階都相同。因為三個動詞都具有相同的主詞，在經濟原則下，省略兩個主詞 forests。此合句的平行結構形式為（主詞＋動詞片語 1＋動詞片語 2, and 動詞片語 3）。同樣地，下列句子

The adult bee fly feeds on flower nectar, <u>but</u> the larvae are parasitic on other insects. 有兩個動詞（fly, are）為兩個句子，主詞不同，加上語意矛盾，使用對等連接詞 but 銜接。此合句的平行結構為（句子 1 ＋ but ＋ 句子 2）。合句的平行結構之詳細說明請參考第七章。

III、複句（Complex Sentence）

複句乃一個敘述句中，包含二個或二個以上獨立的句子，這些句子在整個敘述句中的位階不一。一則為主句，一則為附屬子句。兩者藉助附屬連接詞（when, where, because...）來銜接或組合。附屬子句可分為副詞子句、形容詞子句和名詞子句三種。三大附屬子句的詳細說明請參考第八、九、十章。

例如：

1. Neon is utilized in the airport <u>because it can permeate fog</u>.

此句包括兩個句子，一個主句（Neon is utilized in the airport）和一個副詞子句（it can permeate fog）。兩者呈因果關係，所以透過一個副詞連接詞 because 來銜接。

2. Children who are provided positive feedback for aggressiveness will incorporate this kind of conduct into their behaviors.

此句包括兩個句子，一個主句（Children will incorporate this kind of conduct into their behaviors）和一個形容詞子句（who are provided positive feedback for aggressiveness）。此複句中的子句是修飾主詞（children），所以置於主詞之後，透過形容詞連接詞 who 來銜接。在英文句型中，形容詞片語或形容詞子句，經常置於被修飾字的後面。

3. People believe that a snake's age can be told by counting the rings of its rattles.

此句包括兩個句子，一個主句（People believe）和一個名詞子句（that a snake's age can be told by counting the rings of its rattles）。此複句中的子句作為 believe 的受詞，所以置於動詞，透過 that 副詞連接詞來銜接。

綜合上述的基本英文句子結構的概念，閱讀一個句子時須先判斷主句所在，主要動詞的詞性變化，需和主句主詞單複數一致，不要受修飾語或子句的影響。

例如：The scientific study of the motion of the bodies is called dynamics.

主詞是 study 所以動詞為 is，不要受 of the bodies 的誤導。

>>> **Exercise 1**

Ⅰ、請從以下四個選項中選出正確答案

1. Human brains_____not only our thoughts and conscious actions but also all the unconscious functions of our bodies.
   (A) control
   (B) controlling
   (C) controls
   (D) controlled

2. Some arts _____the historical period during which they were created.
   (A) reflect of
   (B) reflecting
   (C) reflect
   (D) are reflected

3. Any clock _____ by a mainspring must be wound daily or weekly, but electric clocks do not need winding.
   (A) run
   (B) ran
   (C) running
   (D) runned

4. Politics won't occur _____economic stability.
   (A) have no
   (B) do not have
   (C) but no
   (D) without

5. In a sport based upon speed, danger_____ part of the appeal.
   (A) to be
   (B) being
   (C) is
   (D) of being

6. The right to be heard _____ the right to be considered seriously.
   (A) is included   (B) including not
   (C) does not include   (D) including not by

7. A ray of light _____ a thin lens keeps its original direction.
   (A) pass through   (B) passed through
   (C) passes through   (D) passing through

8. _____ applications of the laser beams revolutionized modern medical technologies.
   (A) Although the   (B) The
   (C) It was the   (D) There was the

9. Kimonos are a traditional Japanese costume characterized with _____ _____.
   (A) long, loose robe if wide-sleeved
   (B) robe is long, loose, wide-sleeved
   (C) it is a long loose, wide-sleeved robe
   (D) long, loose, wide-sleeved robe

10. The jet stream is a current of _____.
   (A) air is fast-flowing   (B) air is flowing fast
   (C) fast-flowing air   (D) air flows fast

11. _____ of structure distinguishes the architectural projects of I.M. Pei.
   (A) Integration carefully   (B) The integration is careful
   (C) A carefully integrated   (D) A careful integration

12. All paper is formed into sheets from _____.
    (A) which cellulose fibers   (B) cellulose fibers
    (C) fibers are cellulose   (D) which fibers are cellulose

13. _____ found four-leaf clover is considered a lucky sign.
    (A) It is rarely   (B) Rarely
    (C) The rarely   (D) Despite its being rarely

14. _____ distinguishes jet engines from rocket engines.
    (A) System self-contained by fuel oxidizer
    (B) The self-contained fuel oxidizer
    (C) The System is self-contained fuel oxidizer
    (D) Of self-contained fuel oxidizer

15. _____ coined money dates back to about 3,000 B.C.
    (A) Know to the oldest   (B) It was the oldest known
    (C) Known as the oldest   (D) The oldest known

II、請找出文法錯誤之處，且寫出正確答案

16. Linoleum is waterproof floors covering most made of cloth with a
                            A   B   C

hard shinny substance.
        D

17. The most common form of candle is a hard cylinder of paraffin with a
                              A   B   C
    wick run through its center.
          D

18. The bowl-shaped form of the kettledrum that looks like half of an
        A   B   C   D
    enormous eggshell.

19. The Boston Latin school, the first secondary school in the American
     A   B
    colonies, and started classes in 1635.
                        C   D

20. A loan being acknowledged by a bond, a promissory note or a mere
     A   B   C
    promise to repay.
              D

第二章

名詞
>>> EXERCISE 2

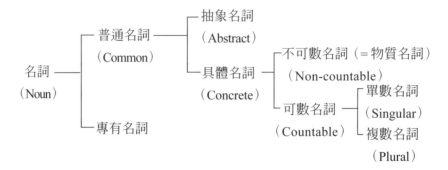

1. According to Herbert J. Muller, instability is one of the conditions of life.
2. Unless we apply the concept of space and time to the impressions we receive, the world is unintelligible.

>>> **Ⅱ、a /an, the 的用法**

1. a /an 的用法：a /an 修飾語的一種，表示「單一」的含意。當被修飾名詞的第一個字母為子音，則採 [a] 如 a program, 10 turns a second, a union, a university（u 發子音）。被修飾名詞的第一個字母為母音，則採 [an] 如 an offer, seventy words an hour.
   (1) Generations of students have learned their economics from Paul A. Samuelson, _____early Nobel Laureate in economics.
   (2) A watt is _____ unit of power equal to the joule per second.
   (3) An able flier, a crow may travel forty miles _____ day before it returns home.
   (4) Eagles have such _____ long, board wings and tails that they look clumsy.
2. the 的用法
   須加上 the 的名詞

(1) 宇宙間獨特的人、事、物或集合：
   the sun/earth/moon/world/sky/universe
(2) 代表群聚之地理名稱：山脈、湖群／海洋、河流、運河／島嶼／地區：
   the Rocky Mountains, the Alps, the Great Lakes, the Atlantic Ocean,
   the Rhine, the Meditteranean Sea, the English Channel, the Panama Canal,
   the Middle East, the Far East, the north of China (northern China)
(3) 概括性名詞：The rose is ... = Roses are...。
(4) 科技發明、儀器或樂器（強調技巧）：the telephone, the guitar。
(5) the ＋國籍：指全體國民，如：the Dutch, the Swiss, the Arabs (are...)。
(6) the ＋形容詞：代表具有此特質的所有人或事：the rich, the unemployed。
(7) 後有修飾之名詞：the capital of New York, the music in the film。

不須加 the 之名詞
(1) 大陸國家或州：Asia, Europe, West Germany, Texas (the United Kingdom, the Republic of Arab Emirates, the United States of America, etc.)。
(2) 城市、街道、鄉村：Cairo, Fifth Avenue, Broadway, New York, Madrid。
(3) 以人名或地名開頭的專有名詞：Kennedy Airport, Cambridge University。

III、字形或字義易混淆的名詞

architecture	architect	economy	economics
editor	editorial	literacy	literature
marriage	mirage	(literate/literary/literal)	
physicist	physician	emergency	emergence
vigor	rigor	poet/poem/poetry	
contain(v.)	content	variable/variety/variation	

IV、特殊名詞

- historian, pedestrian, politician, elite, subordinate, superior
- critic, playwright, scriptwriter, analyst
- architect, professional, amateur, colleague
- athlete, champion, fan, gymnast, rival, hero, heroine, acrobat
- cook, goldsmith, diplomat, official, delegate
- escort, guide, guard, guardian, usher, host, patriot, agent, electorate
- pilgrim, nomad, immigrant, emigrant, migrant, assistant, lieutenant
- explosive, adhesive, relative, representative, additive

V、名詞單複數之判別

1. 單數形，複數意義：指一個單位時，則作單數用；但意指一群人時，作複數用。team, committee, audience, government, faculty, staff, police, *people.
2. 複數形，單數意義：有的名詞看起來像複數，但事實上為單數。
   - 學科：athletics, economics, gymnastics, physics, *statistics,

analgesics, characteristics

　　・疾病名稱：measles（麻疹），mumps（腮腺炎）

　　・一筆錢、一段時間、一段距離：Six miles <u>is</u> too far for me to walk.

　　・其他：amends（賠償），summons（傳票），lens（透鏡，其複數為 lenses）

3. 單、複數同形：fish, deer, a species of, means

　　・Fish _____ no vocal organs but they are by no means silent.

　　・Wealth is a means to an end, not the end itself.

4. 恆為複數：trousers, pajamas, jeans, scissors, spectacles, nippers, pincers。

5. 有些名詞單數、複數的意義不同：

　　・attention 專心 ─────➤ ・attentions 殷勤

　　・confidence 信心 ─────➤ ・confidences 秘密

　　・custom 習俗 ─────➤ ・customs 進口稅

　　・compass 羅盤 ─────➤ ・compasses 指南針

　　・force 力量 ─────➤ ・forces 軍隊

　　・good 好處 ─────➤ ・goods 貨物

　　・honor 榮譽 ─────➤ ・honors 優異成績

　　・letter 字母 ─────➤ ・letters 文學

　　・manner 態度 ─────➤ ・manners 禮節

　　・spectacle 奇觀 ─────➤ ・spectacles 眼鏡

　　・mean 平均中數 ─────➤ ・means 方法

6. 連字號的合併字視為形容詞：

　　・a three-week vacation　　　・a five-man committee

　　・a six-story building　　　・a six-hour journey

7. 有些名詞如前置確定的數目，則視為形容詞片語，其他的情況下，則作代名詞用：

　　・a hundred of, hundreds of,

　　・three dozen eggs,

．dozens of eggs（數＋個）

　．An estimated 10 thousand people are....

8. 有些特殊名詞片語，必須連接複數的名詞：

one of (the candidates); a range of (colors); a variety of (stores); a number of (students), a blend of (elements)

9. 外來名詞依其本國語言的習慣而作不規則的變化：

(1) -us 變 -i   stimulus-stimuli, cactus-_____,

alumnus-_____

(2) -um 變 -a   bacterium-bacteria, medium-_____,

curriculum-_____, datum-_____

(3) -a 變 -ae   alga-algae, larva-larvae

(4) -is 變 -es   crisis-crises, basis-_____,

analysis-_____, thesis-_____,

synopsis-_____, oasis-_____

(5) ix 變 -ices   index-indices, appendix-_____

(6) -on 變 -a   criterion-criteria, phenomenon-_____

(7) -a- 變 -e-   man-men, woman-women (Germans, Romans)

>>> **Exercise 2**

請找出文法錯誤之處，且寫出正確答案

1. According to Buddhism, the simplicity is one of the ideal conditions
   　　A 　　　　　　　　　　B 　　　C
   of sublimed life.
   　　D

2. The space is usually thought of as the empty place that surrounds or
   　　A 　　　　　　　B 　　　　　　　　　　C
   lies between the stars and planets.
   　　D

3. Animal fat exposed to airs becomes a solid substance.
   　　A 　　　B 　　C 　　　　　　　D

4. In an editor, a writer may give his own opinion on a public topic or
   　　　A 　　　　　　　B 　　C
   item of news.
   　　D

5. Most government policies about public affairs have to made on the base
   　　A 　　　　　　　　　　　B 　　　　　　　　　　C
   of extensive surveys and comprehensive discussions.
   　　　D

6. It is essential to develop <u>computer literature</u> in order to find <u>a good job</u>
      A   B   C

   in the modern <u>technological</u> world.
                           D

7. <u>The</u> Taiwan Strait plays <u>a vital role</u> in <u>the maintain</u> of a political
      A   B   C

   balance between Taiwan <u>and</u> Mainland China.
                         D

8. <u>Long exposed</u> to nuclear <u>radiation</u> will cause pregnant women <u>to</u>
        A   B   C

   deliver <u>abnormal</u> or deformed babies.
           D

9. Statistics <u>is</u> a branch of mathematics <u>concerned with</u> <u>the analysize</u> of
        A   B   C

   information expressed <u>in numbers.</u>
                     D

10. <u>In</u> 1993, a total of NT$65 million <u>were</u> spent by visitors <u>on shopping,</u>
       A   B   C

    dinning, lodging, <u>entertainment</u> and transportation.
                          D

11. A micro, an unit of length scientists use to measure very small bits of
        A   B   C
    matter, is about one twenty-five thousandth of an inch.
                                     D

12. A number of researches have called into questions Krashen's language
               A
    learning acquisition theory that L2 learners rely on conscious knowledge
                               B   C
    rather than onlearned knowledge.
               D

13. Malaysia, with more than 4 million Chinese, are considered an ideal
              A   B   C
    place for our overseas investment.
                        D

14. The staff of the Office of Financial Aid are made up of experienced
                                             A
    and knowledgeable experts who are dedicated to help students know
                              B   C
    where financial aid they may qualify for, and directing them in accessing
                                 D
    that help.

15. To keep the class sizes small <u>are to</u> allow <u>faculty members</u> the

                                        A   B

    opportunity <u>to tune in</u> whether or not students understand the material

                      C

    <u>being covered</u>.

          D

16. MIT <u>graduate has</u> earned <u>a reputation for</u> being able to <u>readily</u> apply

           A   B   C

    their knowledge in the business and <u>industrial setting</u>.

                                          D

17. The housing center, a <u>9-stories-high-rise</u> on the south side of campus,

                            A

    contains 142 <u>2 bedroom</u> apartment units, which can <u>house 4 individuals</u>

                       B   C

    and are all air-conditioned, carpeted, and <u>with walk-out balconies</u>.

                                              D

18. <u>In</u> ancient times, native Americans <u>used</u> a variety of <u>shell bead</u> <u>for</u> money.

    A   B   C   D

19. <u>Recently</u>, the USA has suffered <u>an unprecedented</u> series of <u>natural disaster</u>,

       A   B   C

    causing a large amount of loss <u>and deaths</u>.

                                D

20. Harvard Alumni around the world gets together regularly for events
                                      A   B
    ranging from lectures to museum tours to social events.
        C   D

21. A number of United States citizens who are eligible to vote continues
    A   B   C
    to increase.
        D

22. Over the years, the number of corporations and universities have released
      A   B   C

    their technical staff for training in Project SEED.
      D

23. He is a man with a demonstrated ability to work effectively with a
                                              A   B
    wide range of individual and a strong grasp of the issues in the field of
                    C   D
    education today.

24. Gasoline is a fuel of a hundred blends of chemical elements.
            A B   C   D

25. Bloods vessels are narrow tubes through which blood flows in our
         A   B   C   D

   bodies.

26. A five-cent coin is composed by three part copper and one part nickel.
      A   B   C   D

27. In 1992-93, International students at Yale represented 16 percent of
   A   B

   the total students population and came from approximate 50 countries.
                    C   D

28. Iron is incorporated into red bloods cells during their development in
                    A   B   C   D

   the bone marrow.

29. The longest river in the world is Nile, which is 6, 738 kilometers long.
        A   B   C   D

30. The Romans made the lengthy and dangerous voyage across
       A   B

   Mediterranean Sea along the coast of Europe to Great Britain.
          C   D

31. The international Olympic Games, regarded as the world's most
      A   B   C

    prestigious athletic competition, take place once every the four years.
                                                                          D

32. Large number of mercury is used in mixing paints in making explosives
        A   B   C

    and in manufacturing electrical apparatus.
                                         D

33. The focus of an ATLA school will be on integrated curricula that crosses
                                                 A   B

    conventional disciplines, on the active engagement of students in their
                                       C   D

    own learning.

34. Stanford's faculty imbue the school with a ethic that fosters reasoned
                        A   B   C

    dialogue and sound scholarship.
              D

35. *Ulysses*, published in 1922, have no discernible plot, no series of obstacles
                                 A   B

    that a hero or heroine must surmount on the way to a happy ending.
                                                  C   D

36. Thoughts and ideas are communicated by mean of signs, oral language
      A   B   C

and written words.
     D

37. Of the 500 languages that were once spoken by the Chinese, an
estimated _____ today. （請從以下四個選項中選出正確答案）
(A) exist 150   (B) 150 exist
(C) there are 150 exist   (D) 150 existing

38. One of the body's remarkable attributes is to distinguish between their
        A   B   C   D

own and foreign tissues.

39. Although the bite of brown recluse spiders is rarely fatal, they might
                                    A

cause chronic flesh wounds, posing the greatest danger to the infant
                B   C

and elderly.
     D

40. In the U.S.A., clocks are set according to that in the Naval Observatory
               A   B   C

at Washington D.C. .
D

41. Because nickel corrodes slowly, it is widely used for coating other
                           A   B
    metals to protect themselves from rust.
                         C   D

42. Those of us who eat compulsively should follow their doctors'
        A   B   C
    directions to take strict diet plans.
               D

43. One benefit of attending HGSE is the opportunity to enroll in classes
                    A
    conducted by faculty members renowned for his scholarly pursuits
          B   C
    and invigorating teaching styles.
             D

44. What happened in Selma is the effort of American Negroes to secure
          A   B
    for them the full blessings of American life.
        C   D

45. Each year, fires in the U.S.A. cause 12 billion dollars, which are seven
                                  A   B
    times that of Japan on a per capita basis.
           C   D

46. The "Origin of Species" <u>sets out</u> a revolutionary view that <u>the fit</u>, the
                           A   B
    successful, survived to breed; <u>the other</u> over time, <u>died out</u>.
                                   C   D

47. <u>More chemical</u> elements <u>have been</u> discovered by Swedish scientists
        A   B
    than by <u>those</u> of any other <u>countries</u>.
            C   D

48. Linguists believe that gestures <u>were</u> our <u>first form</u> that prehistorical
                                    A   B
    people used <u>to communicate</u> with <u>one the other</u>.
                C   D

49. Like <u>that</u> of any other <u>commodities</u>, the value of diamond <u>results from</u>
         A   B   C
    the interplay of <u>the forces</u> of supply and demand.
                     D

50. The rights of members of the University are not <u>foundamentally</u>
                                                    A
    different <u>from</u> <u>that</u> of <u>other</u> members of society.
              B   C   D

51. Although <u>wood</u> has been <u>considered as</u> the traditional material <u>for</u>
              A   B   C

    <u>construction</u>, several <u>another</u> materials are now used.
                            D

52. Snakes lack the <u>build-in</u> body temperature <u>control</u> many <u>another creatures</u>
                      A   B   C

    <u>possess</u>.
      D

53. Since a tree adds <u>other</u> ring to <u>its</u> trunk every year, age of a tree may be
                     A   B

    calculated <u>by counting</u> the rings <u>on</u> a cross section.
                C   D

54. <u>In times of</u> peace a government may exert pressure on <u>another</u> government,
      A   B

    for political or <u>economic reasons</u>, <u>by mean of</u> an embargo.
                        C   D

55. The relationship of Japanese Katakana <u>to</u> Chinese characters is <u>clearly</u>
                                     A   B

    <u>evident</u> in the <u>written</u> forms that are common <u>to</u> either.
              C   D

第三章

# 動詞 I
>>> EXERCISE 3

>>> I、時態（Tense and Aspect）

1. 不規則的動詞變化
2. 時式與時間副詞一致的原則
   (1) 現在式與過去式的區別：真理、法則及一般的事實。譬如大自然的現象、生物的習性、理化的實驗結果，皆屬一般的原理原則。
      - Objects <u>falling freely</u> in a vacuum <u>had</u> the same rate of speed, <u>regardless of</u> differences in size and weight.
      - The formation of snow must <u>be occurring</u> slowly <u>in calm</u> air, and <u>at</u> temperature near <u>the freezing</u> point.
      - <u>In 1937</u>, Amelia Eathart, the famous aviator, <u>disappears</u> <u>during</u> her attempt <u>to fly</u> around the world.
   (2) 現在完成式與過去完成式的判斷
      - Bone and ivory needles <u>found</u> at archaeological sites <u>indicate</u> <u>that</u> clothes <u>have</u> <u>been sewn</u> for some 17,000 years <u>ago</u>.
      - Adella Prentiss Hughes has <u>served as</u> <u>manager</u> of the Cleverland Orchestra since <u>fifteen years</u>.
3. 一個動詞一個主詞的原則
   - Philosophers commonly <u>reliable on</u> argument <u>to support</u> <u>their</u> own theories and to refute <u>others</u>'.
   - Bats <u>deterministic</u> <u>their position</u> <u>by means</u> of echolocation, a system that does not rely on <u>sight</u>.
   - <u>A</u> Norway rat <u>weights</u> about one pound, and <u>its</u> body is between eight and eighteen <u>inches long</u>.
4. 避免雙動詞的錯誤（V+to-V; V+V-ing）
   (1) V + to-V（不定詞片語）
      agree ask allow decide enable endeavor intend
      tend mean need persuade plan offer remind
      request require appear force

(The function/ objective/ purpose/ aim of ... is to V)

＊to 亦作介系詞用：look forward to/object to/contribute to/ commit to + Ving

(2) V+V-ing（動名詞）

appreciate	complete	consider	delay	enjoy	finish	keep
practice	risk	spend	suggest	quit		

〔例句〕

· The central idea of resource management is to make each action or judgement help achieving a carefully chosen goal.

· When inflation is rampant, many American families find it difficult to maintain the life-style to which they are accustomed.

· The question of the origin of the Moon is interest not only in itself, but as a part of the larger genesis of the Earth and the solar system.

· Mannerist artists tended considering artistic invention and imagination more important than the faithful reproduction of nature.

· Successful economists must have the ability of understanding the effect of world events on national economies.

5. Make, Take , Do 之特殊用法

6. 主詞與動詞一致：

· The ability to retain a mental record of earlier experiences are referred to as "memory".

· Approximately 99 percent of glacier are concentrated in Antarctic and Greenland.

>>> II、主動與被動語態（Active and Passive Voices）

1. 被動語態的動詞沒有受詞，須引入介系詞。

- be +
  - suspected/ashamed/accused/convinced   of
  - accustomed/devoted/dedicated/drawn/sentenced   to
  - fed/filled/crowded/equipped   with
  - engaged/participated   in
  - divided/converted   into
  - forbidden to/kept from/prohibited from

{注意} 授予動詞（ask/tell/offer/give/award/name）的間接受詞當
　　　 主詞時，不須引入介系詞。

- The first prize was awarded to Mary.
- Mary was awarded the prize by the judge.

2. 習慣用語，表示喜悅、悲傷、和驚訝。

- be +
  - annoyed/perplexed/puzzled/pleased   with
  - amazed/surprised/alarmed/astonished/shocked   at
  - disturbed/determined   by
  - tired/ bored/ashamed   of

3. 無 AGENT 的被動語態，常與 as/to be 連用。

- be regarded as
- be agree/appointed to be

- be +
  - acknowledge/interpreted/known/recognized
  - accepted/classified/considered/defined   as + SC (N)
  - taken/dealt with/ referred to /treated   to be (N, adj)
  - characterized/thought of/viewed/described

{注意} 當動作的行為者插入時，as 可以省略。

4. 過去分詞與現在分詞可充當修飾語。

- The ear is an organ ------ (involve) in the perception of sound.
- There was an accident, -------(include) two dead and ten injured.

Exercise 3

1. The decade of the 1960s at HGSE_____ a continued emphasis on
   a comprehensive view of education in social settings.
   (A) witnessing
   (B) is witnessed
   (C) which witnessed
   (D) witnessed

II、請找出文法錯誤之處，且寫出正確答案

2. Genes <u>enable</u> wild plants <u>to resist</u> diseases must continually <u>be transferred</u>
         A   B   C
   to <u>food-producing</u> species to prevent crop failure.
          D

3. The expansion of the right of the individual <u>to behave</u> or misbehave as
                                    A
   <u>he</u> pleases <u>has came</u> at the expense of <u>orderly</u> society.
   B   C   D

4. A national <u>anti-counterfeiting</u> foundation will <u>be inaugurating</u> in the
                     A   B
   first half of next year and will <u>mainly</u> counter <u>piracy</u> of legal software
                          C   D
   programs.

5. Capitalism is <u>an economic</u> and political system <u>in which</u> property
                   A   B

   business and industry <u>are owed</u> by private individuals <u>but not</u> by the state.
                             C   D

6. <u>On</u> the release, Nellie Bly's articles revealing brutal treatment <u>of</u>
     A

   <u>inmates</u>, poor food <u>and and</u> unsanitary conditions <u>leaded to</u> reform.
       B   C   D

7. Descartes' decision <u>regard thoughts</u> rather than external objects as the
                           A

   prime empirical certainties <u>was very important</u>, and <u>had</u> a profound
                                     B   C

   <u>effect on</u> all subsequent philosophy.
       D

8. <u>Tons</u> of boulders <u>were leaved</u> scattered all over <u>what was</u> to become
      A   B   C

   the <u>coastal</u> landscape of Northern Taiwan.
          D

9. A ray of light <u>passing through</u> a thin lens <u>keep</u> <u>its</u> original direction.
    A   B   C D

10. Rightly or wrongly the impression has gain ground abroad that Japan
          A   B   C

    believes in military power as a means of national advancement.
                                         D

11. The subject of pilgrimage should fitted neatly into categories describing
          A   B   C

    history, how it's common to all faiths, etc.
                 D

12. General official records included materials furnished by students, and
                                 A   B

    reference, transcripts and other materials from third parties.
                         C   D

13. The ways in which an individual characteristically acquires, retains,
               A   B

    and retrieves information is collectively termed the individual's
             C   D

    learning style.

14. Nucleus curricula are designed to interweave previous topics into the study
                       A   B

    of new material that reinforces and deeps students' understanding.
                   C   D

15. The number of aeronautical engineers required meeting air transportation
        A   B   C
    needs is rapidly increasing.
          D

16. For his contribution as a journalist to Anglo-American understanding,
    A   B
    Alistair Cooke is made an honorary knight in 1973 by Queen Elizabeth.
                     C   D

17. The blood vessels allowed the continuous circulation of blood to every
                      A   B   C
    organ and tissue of the body.
              D

18. The laser, a fairly recent technological discovery, is an extremely narrow
                A   B
    beam of light, which differs considerably quality from ordinary light.
                                              C   D

19. It's estimated that a country which set higher educational standards for
                                 A
    women has much lower infant mortality rate as well as fertility rate.
          B   C   D

20. Much of the world's commercial supply of tin came from the East
    A   B   C   D
    Indies, Australia & China.

21. The genesis and development of abstract art reflected a desire to
    A   B   C
    express ideas that cannot be expressed in traditional pictorial terms.
                                              D

22. Fish have a well-developed sense of hearing, and the ability of
         A   B   C
    transmitting sound.
         D

23. John William has served as manager of the Machintoshi company
                  A   B   C
    since ten years.
    D

24. In 1984, the world population rose to over 4.7 billion, up almost 85
                                   A   B
    million from an estimate made the year ago.
                  C   D

25. Over the past <u>three decades</u>, murder, rape and <u>violent crime</u> <u>increased</u>
                        A   B   C
    <u>more than</u> 500 percent.
        D

26. The waves of a laser <u>are</u> capable of <u>transmit</u> the messages <u>carried by</u>
                          A   B   C
    telephone, radio and TV <u>combined</u>.
                            D

27. The success of AT&T not only makes <u>itself</u> number one worldwide,
                                        A
    but <u>more importantly</u>, <u>confirms</u> its commitment <u>to satisfy customers</u>.
            B   C   D

28. As a young man, Alexander Graham Bell had dedicated his life <u>to help</u>
                                                                  A
    deaf people and was trying to <u>make extra money</u> by <u>working out</u> how
                                    B   C
    <u>to improve</u> the telegraph.
        D

29. <u>Consume</u> too much sodium <u>is known to</u> contribute to hypertension,
        A   B
    which is a factor <u>in half</u> <u>the deaths</u> in the United States each year.
                        C   D

30. <u>Without</u> the benefit of <u>scientific</u> knowledge, our ancestors had no way
     A   B

   of <u>the knowing of the natural causes</u> of a comets' appearance.
          C   D

31. When a desert storm called the simoon <u>passes</u>, the surface of the
                                        A

   dosert may be so <u>greatly changed that</u> travelers have difficulty
                       B

   <u>to recognize</u> <u>where they are</u>.
       C   D

32. Mary McLeod Bethune spent most of <u>her</u> life <u>work</u> to give <u>other</u> blacks
                              A   B   C

   the chance to read and <u>to learn</u>.
                  D

33. <u>Some</u> special steps <u>are done</u> by the government <u>to improve</u> the current
     A   B   C

   <u>economic</u> situation.
     D

34. American farmers <u>heartily</u> dislike prairie dogs <u>because</u> they <u>make</u> so
                       A   B   C

   much <u>harm</u> to crops.
       D

35. Although adult education in the United States began in colonial times,
    A   B
    the chief growth took place since the 1920's.
                        C   D

36. Bakery products were prepared from flour of meal derived from some
                        A   B   C
    form of grain.
          D

37. Vaporization in connection with general atmospheric conditions have
                    A   B
    a marked effect on long-term climate.
          C   D

38. Although the Weather Bureau and Coast Guard made all they can to
                                                    A   B
    predict and fight hurricanes, the damage each year is tremendous.
            C   D

39. The Field Experience Program provides students the opportunities to
    put theory into practice, take research related to dissertation topics and
                    A   B   C   D
    explore new knowledge.

40. The Ford Company did its debut of the latest model cars last Sunday
　　　A　　　　　　　　　B　C　　　　　　　D
　　in Taipei.

41. The aim of analytic philosophy is correcting the imprecise use of
　　　　　　　　A　　　　　　　　　　B
　　language that causes complex problems.
　　　　　　　　C　　　　D

42. The setting of resource classrooms is increased the numbers of
　　　A　　　　　　　　　　　　　　　　　　B
　　students who graduate with the skills to succeed in the increasingly
　　　　　　　　C　　　　　　　　　　D
　　technological society.

43. So-called freezing point is referred as a point where a liquid becomes
　　　　　　　　A　　　　　B　　　　　　C
　　a solid.
　　D

44. Meteorological cycles have been placed the scrutiny of statisticians
　　　　　　　　　　　A
　　so that recurring patterns not obvious at first sight might be disclosed.
　　　B　　　C　　　　　　　　　　D

45. Since the <u>founding</u> of the United States, <u>most</u> presidents have always

               A   B

    <u>been offered</u> <u>to a second</u> nomination.

        C   D

46. The <u>catfish</u> is the name of <u>a large group</u> of fish, <u>most of which</u> <u>has</u> two

       A   B   C   D

    to four pairs of whiskers.

47. <u>Within</u> our society <u>there</u> still <u>exists</u> rampant nationalism <u>and</u> racism.

     A   B   C   D

III、請從以下四個選項中選出正確答案

48. Confucius was considered by most Chinese in the world _____ greatest educator.

    (A) that he was the   (B) who was the

    (C) by the   (D) the

49. Stephen Hawking is widely regarded by scientists _____ theoretical physicist since Einstein.

    (A) that he is the most   (B) who is the most

    (C) the most   (D) being the most

第四章

# 動詞 II
>>> EXERCISE 4

>>> 語氣（**Mood**）

I. 直述語氣（Indicative Mood）：Did you lift it？

II. 祈使語氣（Imperative Mood）：Don't be silly!/Help yourself!

III. 條件語氣（Conditional Mood）：

   (a) He may get the permission of HGES.

   (b) Drivers should obey the traffic laws.

IV. 假設語氣（Subjective Mood）：顯示說話者強烈的意志、願望、懷疑、要求、建議

1. Subjective that 子句—祈使動詞 / 名詞 + that + (should) + V 原形
   〔祈使動詞〕

ask	advise (-ice)	decide (-cision)
demand	suggest (ion)	determine (-nation)
request	recommend	resolve (- lution)
require (-ment)		
insist	command	
maintain (-tenance)	order	
stipulate (-tion)	regulate (-tion)	

   ・They insisted that we have dinner with them.

   ・The suggestion that Bill take charge of the matter seems reasonable.

   {注意} It be + desirable/essential/urgent/important/necessary + that 子句表必要、緊急，亦視同 that 假設語氣。

2. Subjective if 子句

   (1) indicative if 子句：與現在或未來事實相符；if 子句採簡單現在式

      [If + S1+V1, S2+will/shall+V]

      ・If the temperature goes under below 0℃, water will freeze.

(2) subjective if 子句：與現在事實相悖，if 子句採簡單過去式

[If + S1+V1-ed, S2+would/might+V]

與過去事實相悖，if 子句採過去完成式

[If + S1+had V-en, S2+would have +V-en]

- If there <u>were</u> another world war, the continued existence of human race <u>would be</u> in jeopardy.
- If he <u>had told</u> me about the problem, I <u>would have solved</u> it for him.

3. Subjective wish 子句

I wish that ┌── the war were to stop - 與未來事實相反
            │   I could speak Russian - 與現在事實相反
            └── they could have come - 與過去事實相反

4. As if/as though 如同 ; If only 要是…就好了…
   (1) 推測：
       - They treat me as if I were their son.
       - After this interruption, she carried on taking as if nothing had happened.
   (2) It isn't as if + 假設口氣，難道是… ; 不成。
       - It isn't as if he were poor.（難道他是貧戶不成。）
       - It isn't as if I hadn't not warned him several times.
   (3) If only I knew! (Does the speaker know?)
       - If only the rain would stop! (Does the speaker like the rain?)

5. If...should... (=In case) 萬一
   - If it should rain, can you bring in the washing from the garden?

6. 暗示性假設子句，省略 if 假設子句，以 but 或 without 連接一個事實子句或片語

· I would have helped you, but I had no money.

· I would not have solved the problem without his help.

7. If-omitted 假設子句：將 were, had, should 提到句首

· If I were a bird, ...   → Were I a bird, ...

· If I had known, ...   → Had I known, ...

· If anyone should call ...   → Should anyone call, ...

Exercise 4

I、請找出文法錯誤之處，且寫出正確答案

1. A new skull discovered in Ethiopia <u>strongly suggests</u> that the human
                                               A

   family tree <u>have</u> one root; the species Australopithears Afarensis,
                 B

   which lived just after <u>the human</u> and ape lineages <u>splitted</u>.
                          C   D

2. <u>It</u> is essential that environmental pollution <u>is</u> controlled and <u>eventually</u>
   A   B   C

   <u>eradicated</u>.
          D

3. The law I <u>am referring</u> to requires that anyone who <u>owns</u> a house <u>has</u>
              A   B   C

   <u>fire insurance</u>.
          D

4. <u>The Constitution</u> provides that all people <u>are entitled</u> <u>to</u> equal
          A   B   C

   protection <u>under</u> the law.
              D

5. It is <u>desirable</u> that violations of <u>privacy</u>, such as <u>monitoring</u> mail and

          A   B   C

    phone conversation, searching persons and their property <u>are outlawed</u>.

                                                        D

6. It's <u>extremely</u> important that <u>every</u> civilian <u>has</u> the freedom of

          A   B   C

    religion, speech, press, <u>assembly</u> and association.

                          D

7. The prisoner obtains <u>a commutation</u> of his sentence <u>on</u> condition that

                              A   B

    he <u>find</u> a job and <u>stays out</u> of trouble six months.

          C   D

8. It is obviously urgent that we <u>be aware</u> of the impact of <u>golfing boom</u>,

                                 A   B

    which <u>has grown</u> <u>enough severe</u> to destroy our living environment.

                C   D

II、請從以下四個選項中選出正確答案

9. If blood _____ from the stomach right after a meal, digestion of
food will be hampered.
   (A) has been transferred   (B) were transferred
   (C) will be transferred   (D) is transferred

10. If the largest comet _____ Earth head on, we could notice only a shower of meteors.

(A) is stricken   (B) would be stricken

(C) strikes   (D) were to strike

11. _____ in transportation, medieval Europe could not have adopted monetary units of exchange and eliminated the process of bartering

(A) If there was no improvements

(B) Had there been no improvements

(C) If there were no improvements

(D) If there hadn't had improvements

12. Were the ice of Greenland and Antarctic to melt, the sea level _____ at least 100 feet.

(A) would have risen   (B) would rise

(C) will have risen   (D) had risen

13. The fact that the Earth revolved around the sun _____ had Galileo not cared passionately about truth and delighted in proving the errors and absurdities of the beliefs of his time.

(A) might not have been proved   (B) might not be proved

(C) had been proved   (D) was proved

14. The flowers would have grown well but Eva _____ them.

(A) always forgot to water   (B) hadn't water

(C) hasn't watered   (D) wouldn't have watered

III、請找出文法錯誤之處，且寫出正確答案

15. If Danile hadn't failed <u>in training</u> for <u>long-distance</u> running, he <u>would be</u>
                          A   B   C

   able to finish <u>the 26-mile</u> Boston Marathon.
                      D

16. Had the British <u>not imposed</u> a <u>tax on</u> tea imported by the American
                        A   B

   Colonies, the colonists <u>might not rebel</u>, <u>starting</u> the American revolution.
                         C   D

17. If <u>more rain</u> <u>fell throughout</u> the South West during 1979, <u>thousands of</u>
     A   B   C

   animals might not have <u>died for</u> lack of water.
                  D

18. The <u>theoretical existence</u> of the planet could not be determined if
           A

   erratic <u>variations</u> <u>hadn't occurred</u> in the <u>orbits</u> of Uranus and Neptune.
            B   C   D

19. If only you <u>are</u> a little more <u>concerned</u> <u>about</u> me.
            A   B   C   D

20. The Hopi dancers, holding rattle snakes in their mouths, may be bitten
      A   B   C

   by the snakes but they continue as if nothing happens.
                                              D

21. Few blankets made by South native Taiwanese would have survived
     A

   to the present were it not due to enthusiastic collectors at the turn of
        B   C   D

   the century.

22. How will our pattern of life be altered if we did not have written or
        A   B   C

   spoken language?
     D

23. If techniques can be created for achieving internal happiness, modern
                   A   B   C

   society would be far more advanced.
               D

24. With the increase of automation, the problems of unemployment will
     A

   become more serious unless more people would be given the training
           B   C   D

   necessary for white collar position.

25. His report <u>would be</u> released last year if new researches had not made

            A

    it necessary <u>to revise</u> all conclusions <u>drawn from</u> his <u>first series of</u>

                B   C   D

    experiments.

[Ving, V-en 分詞之運用]

26. Geologists believed that the Baling land bridge <u>disappeared</u> about

                                                    A

    14,000 years ago, <u>when</u> massive glaciers melted, <u>caused</u> the sea level

                        B   C

    to rise <u>several hundred</u> feet worldwide.

                 D

27. The impressionists were <u>mainly</u> concerned with the study of light <u>and</u>

                            A   B

    color, <u>seek to</u> capture <u>the reality</u> of a particular moment.

               C   D

28. The characteristics of optics <u>are</u> the <u>well arrange hues</u> and geometric

                                 A   B

    <u>patterns</u> that create optical <u>illusions</u>.

       C   D

29. <u>Vegetable</u> oil is triglyceride oil typically <u>extracting</u> from <u>the seeds</u> of

      A   B   C

    soy, peanut, cotton, sunflower <u>and other plants</u>.

                               D

30. The actual quantity of folic acid is required in the daily diet is unknown.
　　　A　　　　　　　　　　　　　　　B　　　　　C　　　　D

31. Marine biology, the study of oceanic plants and animals and their
　　　　　　　　　　　　　　　　A　　　　　　　　　　　　B
　　ecological relationships, has farthered the efficient development of
　　　　　　　　　　　　　　　　C
　　fisheries.
　　　D

32. The largest of the nine planets, Jupiter is a gigantic ball of hydrogen
　　　A
　　and helium with a small core that may be made mostly of a metallic
　　　　　　　　　　B　　　　　　　　　　　　C　　　　　　　　　　　D
　　hydrogen slush.

33. Pilots rarely concentrate on the one particular instrument on the flight
　　　　　A　　　　　　　　　　　　　　B
　　desk, but rather checked them all at intervals.
　　　　　　　　　C　　　　　　　D

34. Climatic conditions variable considerably in Utah, largely because of
　　　A　　　　　　　　B　　　　　　　　　　　　　　C
　　differences in latitude and elevation.
　　　D

35. James Baldwin's just *Above My Head* is a <u>revealing</u> book <u>portrays</u> all
                                                 A   B

the lyricism, violence, and <u>tenderness</u> that <u>contribute to</u> human interaction.
                                        C   D

第五章

形容詞與副詞

>>> EXERCISE 5

皆作修飾語（modifiers）用，形容詞修飾名詞或代名詞；副詞則修飾動詞、形容詞、其他副詞或整個句子。

drastical change/change drastically, absolute ignorance/ absolutely right

>>> **II、種類**

1. 形容詞的字尾經常是 -ous, -ful, -ic, -ent, -ate, -ish, -ary, -ive, -able, 這些形容詞一般加上 -ly，就形成情狀副詞。
   - original/ordinary/fortunate/reluctant/available/artificial/competent harmful/snobblish/effective/marvelous

   {注意} 名詞 -ly → ADJ: earthly/worldly/yearly/lovely/elderly

2. 形、副同形：fast/early/late/hard/near/enough/high/yearly/daily。

3. 複合形容詞：兩個或兩個以上的字的組合，字與字之間以「-」連接。
   - 名詞─分詞：a bowl-shaped kettle, an earth-covered shelter, coal-producing swamps, a world-shaking affair。
   - 副詞─動詞 - ed：well-educated, long-wound。
   - 形容詞─名詞 - ed：slant-roofed, long-armed, one-eyed。

4. 名詞作形容詞用：a law teacher/ opera tickets, silk shirts, folk music。

>>> **III、動詞分詞：V-ing, V-ed**

V-ing 和 V-ed 可視為動詞的衍生字，作為形容詞之用。受修飾名詞具有某種行為能力，則以 V-ing 修飾之，例如：a singing bird, a girl dancing on TV。受修飾名詞具為接受某行為者，則以 V-ed 修飾之。例如：a broken heart, a book written in English。兩者可做前位或後位修飾。

IV、選字

- like/alike/likely
- personal/personnel
- not/no/none
- most/almost/mostly
- dead/deadly
- hard/hardly
- late/lately
- desirable/desirous
- interesting/interested
- sensible/sensitive
- wooded/wooden
- some/somewhat
- alive/living
- honorable/honorary
- several/severally
- high/highly
- respectful/respective
- near/nearly/nearby
- enviable/envious
- industrial/industrious
- alone/lonely

>>> Exercise 5

I、請從以下四個選項中選出正確答案

1. It is difficult to realize that a piranha fish only 30 centimeter long could be a _____ threat to a human being.
   (A) dead   (B) deadly
   (C) death   (D) died

2. When you eat _____, you get the vitamins you need from the foods you eat.
   (A) a diet of well balance (B) to balance a diet
   (C) a diet is well balance (D) a well-balanced diet

3. In 1911, a scientist in Poland found that the reason beriberi was occurring _____ in the Orient was that people there ate mainly white or polished rice.
   (A) almost   (B) almostly
   (C) the most   (D) mostly

4. Born into the _____ classes of Victorian London, Charles Spencer Chaplin was faced with homelessness, hunger, alcoholism in the workhouse.
   (A) the poverty of strictness. (B) stricting-poverty
   (C) to strict poverty   (D) poverty-stricten

II、請找出文法錯誤之處，且寫出正確答案

5. Many <u>high corrosive</u> acids do not <u>affect</u> titanium, <u>a</u> lightweight, <u>silver-gray</u>
            A   B   C   D
metal.

6. Pekingese <u>is</u> a toy dog <u>of a breed</u> developed in China, <u>having</u> a flat
              A   B   C
nose, a <u>hair-long</u> coat and short legs.
            D

7. After <u>experimenting with</u> gliders for years, the Wright brothers
                  A
<u>became convinced</u> that a <u>drive-power</u> machine was necessary for <u>flying</u>.
       B   C   D

8. A <u>thimble-shape</u> cup of wood and hair <u>fastened to</u> a twig <u>is</u> the
        A   B   C
<u>humming bird's</u> nest.
        D

9. Although there are <u>a</u> number of different kinds of <u>producing-wool</u>
                   A   B
sheep, merino sheep <u>are</u> the most <u>extensively known</u>.
                C   D

10. Shortages of food <u>made</u> the Americans <u>anxious</u>, <u>particular</u> under the
                  A   B   C

present conditions of <u>perceived worldwide</u> deficiencies.
                            D

11. It's hard <u>to imagine</u> that the head of a comet may be <u>over</u> a <u>million</u>
              A   B   C

kilometers <u>in wide</u>.
        D

12. In ancient times, people used <u>the notched sticks</u> <u>in combination with</u>
                                      A   B

the knotted strings of different <u>long</u> <u>that stood for</u> certain things.
                                       C   D

13. <u>Estimates</u> of the number of pigeons went <u>as high as</u> nine <u>million</u> but
     A   B   C

now there are <u>no</u>.
           D

14. <u>Pollen grains</u> <u>are</u> usually about 25 micros <u>across</u> and spores are <u>some</u>
     A   B   C   D

smaller.

15. Although an <u>acoustically excellent</u> music hall cannot make an

                                        A

   orchestra <u>sound better</u> than <u>it is really</u>, it can allow it <u>to reach</u> its

                 B   C   D

   potential unhindered.

16. Myna birds are <u>rich colored</u>, <u>varying from</u> dark reddish-brown to

                       A   B

   black, <u>with white-tipped</u> wings and bright yellow <u>legs and bills</u>.

                    C   D

17. <u>Any</u> democratic election champions should be <u>conducted</u> <u>in</u> an <u>orderly</u>

   A   B   C

   <u>and equitably</u> way.

          D

18. The torpedo fish <u>is</u> noted <u>almost</u> for its ability <u>to generate</u> electricity

                    A   B   C

   and <u>to give</u> electric shocks.

          D

19. When <u>other communications</u> fail, carrier pigeons, which are swift and

                 A

   small, <u>are</u> likely to arrive <u>safe</u> at their destination.

          B   C D

20. Nuclear power plants <u>current</u> provide about <u>8 percent</u> of <u>the</u> electricity

                             A   B   C

    <u>generated</u> in the U.S.

        D

21. I have a dream that this nation will live out the true meaning of <u>its</u>

                                                             A

    creed: We hold these <u>truths</u> to be <u>self-evident</u>: that all men are created

                           B   C

    <u>equally</u>.

        D

22. With her <u>expressive</u> Italian voice <u>enhanced with</u> <u>animated-intensely</u>

                 A   B   C

    gestures, Dr. Montessori displayed a strong talent <u>for public speaking</u>.

                                                    D

23. Natural pigments <u>are</u> <u>primarily</u> of <u>animals</u> and vegetable <u>origins</u>.

                      A   B   C   D

24. Proteins form <u>the most</u> of <u>the substances</u> of food, <u>such as</u> eggs, meat,

                   A   B   C

    and <u>milk</u>, etc.

        D

25. An average golf court consumes 6,500 cubic meters of water per day,
          A   B

    which is enough sufficient to meet the needs of 6,000 people in the
                         C   D

    Thai capital.

26. Rene Descartes is considered usually the founder of modern
                           A

    philosophy, for he did not accept foundations laid by predecessors, but
                                            B

    endeavored to construct an entirely new one
         C   D

27. By the sixth century, there had been a heavy flow of cultural influences
     A   B   C

    into China from the near continent.
                         D

28. Delicams are large, web-foot water birds, widely distributed in warm
                             A   B

    regions, and often seen along the shore of seas.
              C   D

29. It was Leonardo da Vinci's <u>incomparative</u> power of <u>abstraction</u>,

                                       A   B

    <u>combined with</u> his powerful eye for details, <u>that</u> made him a great

              C   D

    anatomist.

30. Read the final paragraph <u>or two</u>, <u>which</u> will give you <u>a summary</u> of

                                 A   B   C

    the material <u>covering</u>.

                  D

31. Men are <u>typical</u> motivated by <u>a</u> social structure <u>that</u> says if you don't

                A   B   C

    dominate, you will <u>be dominated</u>.

                      D

32. Mountain lions are <u>so geared</u> for a life <u>lonely</u>, and each inclines so

                        A   B

    <u>sedulously</u> to solitude that they rarely fight <u>one another</u>.

        C   D

33. <u>Years-long</u> Renaissance voyages around the world can now be made

      A

    at leisure in a few months, and <u>hurried in</u> 40 hours.

                               C D

      B

34. Garden and landscape design is unique concerned with direct relations
                                A   B   C
    among art, science and nature.
       D

35. Near half of the ancient meteor craters have been found in central and
      A   B   C
    eastern Canada.
       D

36. The water in Lake Superior is mostly totally pure, with only localized
       A   B   C   D
    areas of pollution.

37. Not like jams, which contain fruit pulp, jellies are prepared from strained
       A   B   C   D
    fruit juice.

38. During the seventeenth century, the most colonists were primarily
       A   B
    concerned with economics and defense.
                  C

39. Although thinking cannot be <u>observed direct</u>, psychologists can <u>make</u>
                                      A   B

assumptions about it <u>by studying</u> the relationship between problem
                          C

<u>and response</u>.
      D

40. Fluorine <u>combines with</u> <u>other elements</u> <u>more ready</u> than any other
                    A   B   C

<u>chemical element</u>.
      D

第六章

There, It

>>> EXERCISE 6

>>> I、引介字（There）

【功能】

如果主詞沒有 DET（the/these/that/those/ 所有格），用 there +
be 來引介，相當於中文的「有」，指「存在」，非「所有權」。
充當功能性主詞。

{注意} they are/there are 的差別（there +「數量」的名詞片語）

・There is a mass rally in front of the Presidential Building.

・There was an agreement between the boss and the employees.

>>> II、虛字（It）

【功能】

1. 虛主詞：主詞是不定詞、動名詞或名詞子句時。

　・To quit smoking is advisable.

　・That the construction of the mass rapid transit system will end
　　before the New Year is a good news.

　・Walking along at midnight in this area is unwise.

2. 虛受詞：

　・We all considered it a pity that you couldn't come with us.

　・We believe it wrong to cheat in exam.

　・You will find it interesting playing this new computer game.

3. 特定用法：

　・It happened that/It is likely that/It proved that/It occurred to me
　　that

III、分裂句（Cleft Sentence）

【功能】強調句型；除動詞外，強調句中的任何部分（主詞、受詞、副詞片語）。

1. 強調主詞、受詞
   - I solved this math problem with great difficulty.
   - It was I who(that) solved this math problem with great difficulty.
   - It was this math problem that I solved with great difficulty.

2. 強調副詞片語：尤其 only 和「not until」。
   - It was only when he left school that he realized the importance of studying English.
   = It was not until he left school that he realized the importance of ...

Ⅰ、請從以下四個選項中選出正確答案

1. _____ 290 recognized species of pigeons in the world.
   (A) About   (B) For about
   (C) About the   (D) There are about

2. It is estimated that _____ may be several thousand languages and
   dialects spoken in the world.
   (A) they   (B) there
   (C) it   (D) what

3. _____ different methods people use to communicate with one
   another.
   (A) Several   (B) There are many
   (C) There being many   (D) The many

4. _____ theories have been advanced to account for the existence of
   the moon.
   (A) They have many   (B) There have been many
   (C) Many   (D) That many

5. _____ an estimated one million American women having received
   silicone breast implants.
   (A) There are   (B) It is
   (C) Approximately   (D) That

6. It is only _____ developed that people began trying to record their messages, their experiences and their ideas.

   (A) oral communication was   (B) after oral communication was

   (C) that oral communication was   (D) if oral communication was

7. _____ that Quinine, the drug which is extracted from cinchona bark, was widely used as medicine.

   (A) It was not until 1816   (B) Not until it was 1816

   (C) Not until in 1816   (D) Until it was in 1816

8. It was _____ the Greeks had built up an alphabet of 24 letters, including 5 vowels acquired from the Phoenicians.

   (A) by about 800 B.C. that

   (B) when about 500 B.C.

   (C) the time when was about 800 B.C.

   (D) the time by about 800 B.C. is

9. It was Cillian Gilbreth _____ to make them work more effectively in the early 1900s.

   (A) to study workers' motions   (B) who studied workers' motions

   (C) studies workers' motions   (D) by studying workers' motions

10. _____ the Greeks had coined money more than 2,600 years ago.

   (A) Evident   (B) It is evidence that

   (C) There is evidence that   (D) Evidence is of

11. It is _____ leather its permeability to air and water vapor.
   (A) the structure it gives
   (B) giving it the structure of
   (C) structure that gives it
   (D) its structure that gives

12. _____ Vermont, threatened with invasion, declared itself an independent commonwealth.
   (A) In 1777 that it was
   (B) It was in 1777 that
   (C) Because in 1777
   (D) That in 1777

13. _____ that the formation of the sun, the planets, and other stars began with the condensation of an interstellar gas cloud.
   (A) Believing
   (B) To believe
   (C) The belief
   (D) It is believed

II、請找出文法錯誤之處，且寫出正確答案

14. It was during the latter part of the 19th century the university began to boom,
                          A   B   C
   enrollment rising from 100 to 3,000.
                      D

15. Traditionally, there has been only two major political parties in the
          A   B   C
   United States the Republicans and the Democrats.
                                                    D

第七章

# 合句
>>> EXERCISE 7

合句乃一個以上的簡單句平行組合而成的對等子句。這兩個句子在整個敘述句中的分量同等，藉助對等連接詞（but, or, and, yet）來銜接或組合。連接詞兩邊可能是對稱的兩個子句、兩個動詞片語、兩個名詞片語或介系詞片語。合句一般以平行結構的型態出現。

（主詞＋述詞）＋對稱連接詞＋（主詞＋述詞）

	not (only)...but (also)	
子句 1	(both)...and	＋子句 2
	(either/neither)...or/nor	

· The adult bee fly feeds on flower nectar, <u>but</u> the larvae are parasitic on of her insects.（子句－子句）
· Parrots form couples <u>and</u> often stay mated for life.（片語－片語）
· There are three types of galaxy: spiral, elliptical, <u>and</u> irregular.（名詞－名詞）

>>> **Exercise 7**

1. The Romans adopted the Greek alphabet, perfected it, and _____ to later people.
   (A) it was passed it on   (B) passed it on
   (C) passing it on   (D) to pass it on

2. Most scholars see power and leadership as not things _____ relationship.
   (A) either   (B) or
   (C) with   (D) but

3. Let every nation know that we should pay any price, _____ and oppose any force to assure the success of liberty.
   (A) which bears any burden   (B) bearing any burden
   (C) burden-born   (D) bear any burden

4. There is evidence that solar energy either is now economically competitive with conventional sources of heat _____ so within a few years.
   (A) will be or   (B) but will be
   (C) or will be   (D) and it will be

5. The reconstruction of South Africa will require not just huge amount of funds but also _____.
   (A) they implement with techniques
   (B) they need techniques to implement
   (C) techniques needed in their implementation
   (D) with techniques to implement

6. A dulcimer can be played either by striking its strings with a hammer or _____.
   (A) to pluck them with fingers   (B) fingers are used to pluck them
   (C) they are plucked with fingers (D) by plucking them with fingers

7. Most parents of juvenile offenders rarely impoverished but have a high incidence either of divorce _____ rigid morality.
   (A) and   (B) and of
   (C) or   (D) or of

8. The clay burial vessels from the Chou Dynasty are decorated with zigzag, grooved, and _____.
   (A) geometrically designed   (B) designs are geometric
   (C) geometric designs   (D) geometry designed

9. The skeleton of a person or an animal is the framework of bones, whose exterior layer is smooth, dense continuous, and _____.
   (A) of varying thickness   (B) varied thickness
   (C) its thickness varies   (D) its thickness, varying

10. _____ hasten wrinkling of the skin, but it apparently interferes with the healing process after a face lift.

(A) Smoking not only　　　　　(B) Not only does smoking

(C) It is smoking　　　　　　　(D) Smoking

II、請找出文法錯誤之處，且寫出正確答案

11. The term "moral leadership" <u>introduced in</u> James M. Burns' means
A

that leaders and followers have a relationship <u>not only</u> of power but <u>to</u>
B

<u>mutual needs</u>, aspiration <u>and values</u>.
C　　　　　　　　D

12. <u>The prospect</u> of a new way of automobile <u>imports</u> has promoted
A　　　　　　　　　　　　　　　　B

domestic manufactures <u>to</u> reduce staff, close plants and <u>offering</u>
C　　　　　　　　　　　　　　　D

buyers financial incentives.

13. <u>Not only</u> because of the high caliber of its students but also <u>for the</u>
A

<u>desirable location</u> and climate, Stanford has attracted <u>to its faculty</u>
B　　　　　　　　　　　　　　　　　　　C

some of the <u>world's most</u> respected scholars.
D

14. By 1914, ten of western states had granted women the right to vote,
                                              A   B

    but only one in the East was.
                   C   D

15. Some symbolic decorations often found on traditional architectural
                                   A   B
    details create an air of nostalgia as well as beautiful.
                    C   D

16. To be an effective writer, one should be able to write what he wishes
    A   B
    to say with clear, directness and economy.
             C   D

17. Why does time never go backward? The answer lies not in the laws of
                                                A   B
    nature, except in the conditions prevailing in the early universe.
            C   D

18. Instead of glorious plumage, the peahen, a female peacock, is usually
    A
    colored a dull brown and has either fan nor crest.
    B   C   D

19. The rattle snake <u>strikes quickly</u>, <u>burying</u> its fangs and injects <u>its</u> poison
                      A   B   C

    <u>into</u> the victim.
     D

20. The majority of cans are <u>rarely</u> tin and are made of <u>such other metals</u>
                                 A   B

    as iron and steel <u>and then</u> <u>coating with</u> tin.
                      C   D

21. Industrial pollution <u>has done</u> <u>seriously</u> and possibly irreversible damage
                           A   B

    <u>to</u> the bronze horses <u>on the façade</u> of the Cathedral of St. Mark in Venice.
    C   D

22. <u>An</u> individual joins a community <u>ideally characterized</u> by free expression,
    A   B

    <u>free inquire</u>, intellectual honesty and respect for the dignity of <u>the others</u>.
           C   D

23. <u>Over</u> the years, <u>countless</u> storytellers have been narrating tales <u>that entertain</u>
    A   B   C

    their listeners as well as <u>teaching them</u> a lesson.
                              D

24. Accidents <u>at work</u> usually occur either because equipment is dangerous
　　　　　　　A

or <u>because of</u> their workers are not trained <u>to do</u> jobs <u>correctly</u>.
　　　B　　　　　　　　　　　　　　　　　　　C　　　　　D

25. <u>Architect</u> Frank Lloyd Wright <u>believed that</u> a building should be
　　　A　　　　　　　　　　　　　　　B

designed <u>to fit</u> its function and <u>it is</u> located.
　　　　　C　　　　　　　　　D

26. <u>Either</u> increases and decreases in <u>the amount of</u> glacier ice would
　　A　　　　　　　　　　　　　　　　　B

<u>adversely affect</u> the distribution of people and their <u>economic relationships</u>.
　　C　　　　　　　　　　　　　　　　　　　　D

27. Salt Lake City, <u>Utah's</u> capital and <u>largest city</u>, is <u>an</u> <u>industry</u> and
　　　　　　　　　　A　　　　　　　　　　B　　　　C　　D

banking center.

28. Unlike <u>most leading writers</u> of his time, Henry David Thoreau came
　　　　　　A

from a family <u>which was</u> neither <u>wealth</u> <u>nor</u> distinguished.
　　　　　　　B　　　　　　　C　　D

29. A rat's <u>sharp teeth</u> can gnaw plaster, wood or <u>soft metallic</u> <u>such as</u> <u>lead</u>.
　　　　　A　　　　　　　　　　　　　　　B　　　　C　　D

30. Not only <u>artificial reefs</u> provide fish <u>with food</u> and shelter, but <u>they</u>
              A   B   C
    also serve as <u>important underwater landmarks</u>.
                          D

第八章

# 副詞子句
>>> EXERCISE 8

>>> I、結構

1. 限定子句（Finitive C）
   - When Congress passed the Yellowstone Act, the world first national park was created.
2. 分詞構句（Non-finitive C）：其主詞是暗示性的，與主要子句的主詞相同，被省略掉。
   - Endeavoring to form his own orchestra for many years, Glenn Miller achieved world fame in 1939 as a big band leader.
   - Once threatened with extinction, the trumpet swan has made a strong comeback in the national parks of the U.S.A. .
3. 省略句（Mitted C）
   - Keenly aware of the advantages of a college education, many young people study very hard to obtain it.
   - Although poisonous, many alkaloids（鹼性物質）are valued as medicine.
4. 介系詞片語／介系詞子句（Pre Ph/Pre C）
   - Despite inflation, the standard of living in Taiwan has risen during the past decade.
   - With the coming of spring, his health is improved. (= When spring comes, ...)

>>> II、連接性副詞：非連接詞，不能連接兩個子句

1. However, nevertheless（然而）：有連接詞 but 的意味。
   - He is nice; however, I don't like him.
   - His is nice. Nevertheless, I don't like him.
2. therefore, thus（因此）：有連接詞 so 的意味，表示兩個句子間邏輯的關係。

   then（然後）：有連接詞 and 的意味，表示兩個句子發生前後次

序的關係。

・She is the only candidate; <u>therefore</u> she was elected.

・He studied hard <u>and thus</u> he got good grades.

・I had a shower <u>and then</u> went to bed.

3. moreover, furthermore, besides, in addition（此外）：有連接詞 and 的意味。

・She dances well;　furthermore,　she is good at singing.
　　　　　　　　　　moreover,
　　　　　　　　　　in addition,

⟫⟫⟫ III、功能及其副詞連接詞

1. 時間副詞子句

(1) when/while/since/as …當／當…的時候／自…之後／當（強調兩個連續的動作）

・He left when I arrived.

・A neutron forms when a star much more massive than the sun dies and explodes.

・Strike while iron is hot.

・I stayed there while the meeting lasted.

・I have been there many times since the war ended.

・As they walked along the street, they looked into the window.

・I had to leave just as the conversation was getting interesting.

・I began to enjoy the job more just as I got used to it.（逐漸…）

(2) until/not until....

(a) 在肯定句中，作「直到」解，後接時間片語時，可省略 it was。

・He will be away until Monday.（他將在星期一當天回來。）

・He waited until the sun set.

‧ Dried leaves continue to hang on the branches of some deciduous trees until the new leaves appear.

(b) 用在否定句中，指「在…之前」，有 before 的意思。

‧ Until then, I knew nothing at all about it.

‧ The baby didn't stop crying until he was fed.

‧ Washington was not honored with a coin until the bicentennial of his birth.

(c) not until 置於句首時，主句須倒裝。

‧ Not until they defeated the British army in 1776 did the American colonies declare it independence.

2. 地方副詞子句：where/wherever/where...there

‧ Wherever we went, we found poverty.

‧ Where Jones works, there you will find the root of the problem.

‧ Where there is a will, there is a way.

‧ Where there is no rain, farming is difficult or impossible.

3. 條件、讓步副詞子句

(1) although/though/even though(if) + 子句 …雖然，儘管。

in spite of / despite + 名詞片語

‧ Although she smokes 40 cigarettes a day, she is quite fit.

‧ I didn't get the job even though (= though) I had all the necessary qualification.

‧ In spite of (=Despite) the heavy traffic, I arrived on time.

(2) unless + 子句 / except (for) + 名詞片語，…除非。

‧ Unless he is fired, I will quit.

‧ Except John, all of my students attended the lecture.

(3) No matter …無論如何。

[no matter ＋ how ＋形容詞＋子句（主詞＋動詞）]

‧ No matter how unimaginable it may be, we cannot know both the position and the velocity of an electron at the same time.

‧ However sympathetic the white men might be, it is difficult for them to evaluate Indian art.

[No matter + what + 名詞 + 子句（主詞 + 動詞）]

・No matter what language it is written in, what is original will be read.

(4) whether...or not 無論如何。

　・Whether he is right or wrong, he always comes off worst in argument.

4. 因果關係副詞子句：because/since/as/ for/in that + 子句
　　　　　　　　　　because of/on account of + 名詞片語 ⎤因為。

・Nevada has limited supply because of (= on account of) its light rainfall.

・As (=Since) he was broke, he committed suicide.

・Helium is safer than hydrogen because it can not explode.

5. 狀況副詞連接詞：seeing (that)/now that... 既然，因為，鑑於。

・Your son reads well, seeing that he has attended school so short a time.

6. 目的副詞連接詞：in order to / so as to 為了。

・To improve our minds, we must read more books of high intellectual quality.

I、請從以下四個選項中選出正確答案

1. Although _____ some electric products, it imports many as well.
   (A) the exporting of Taiwan   (B) exporting from Taiwan
   (C) Taiwan exports   (D) Exporter of Taiwan

2. _____ the increasing price for drugs, western chemists are experimenting with herbs used for many centuries in Asian medical practice.
   (A) They confront with   (B) That they confront with
   (C) Confronted with   (D) The confrontation with

3. Often guided by traditional healers, _____ world wide in search of cures or treatments for ailments ranging from AIDS to the common colds.
   (A) rain forests are combined by scientists
   (B) scientists are combining rain forests
   (C) the combination of rain forests
   (D) scientists combining rain forests

4. _____, Martin Luther King led his supporters in dramatic non-violent campaigns for civil rights of black people in the U.S.A. .
   (A) Influenced by the writings of Gandhi
   (B) The influence of Gandhi's writings
   (C) That was the influence of Gandhi's writings
   (D) What was influenced by Gandhi's writings

5. It is said that extreme poverty forces some people to steal, _____ it is obvious that some people from rich family will commit crimes.

   (A) where   (B) in that
   (C) thus   (D) whereas

6. Mikhail Gorbachev brought the Soviet people the freedom to break through and the freedom to speak one's mind _____ he did not bring them the prosperity they so desperately need.

   (A) and then   (B) later
   (C) but   (D) so that

7. _____ , the existing law is adequate to deal with the dangerous motor driver.

   (A) Properly enforced   (B) It is properly enforced
   (C) To enforced properly   (D) Despite properly enforce

8. Prospective international students must demonstrate adequate support _____ to enter the U.S.A. .

   (A) they should receive a visa   (B) before receiving a visa
   (C) that they have received a visa (D) which is received a visa

9. In Russia, _____ , all vegetables except for potatoes and the pervasive cabbages in soup seem to disappear from the menu.

   (A) winter approaches
   (B) winter's approaching
   (C) because the approaching winter
   (D) as winter approaches

10. Magnesium is peculiarly light and, _____ properly combined with other metals, very strong and durable.
(A) if
(B) has
(C) and
(D) that

11. _____ you can buy the same brand of soap, toothpaste and sugar-free carbonated drink in all 50 states, the United States reveals major regional differences.
(A) How
(B) In spite of
(C) Because
(D) Although

12. _____ their many differences of literary perspectives, Emerson, Thoreau, Hawthorne and Whiteman share certain beliefs: humans are the spiritual center of the universe.
(A) Despite
(B) Although
(C) Since
(D) Because of

13. _____, a tornado comes into contact with a much smaller area, but it is much evident and destructive.
(A) Comparing a cyclone
(B) A cyclone with comparison to
(C) Compared to a cyclone
(D) A cyclone to be compared with

14. It is well to keep away from a snake _____ you can be positive that it is not poisonous.
(A) except for
(B) but
(C) unless
(D) only

15. _____ a total population of less than one hundred and fewer breeding females than ever, the Indian rhino seemed to be in danger of disappear.
    (A) The   (B) Because
    (C) Consequently   (D) With

16. _____ discovery of vaccination, small box, a fatal disease, in 18th century has been practically wiped out
    (A) The   (B) Whereas
    (C) Only the   (D) With the

17. _____ trying to enrich her inner-self, a modern Japanese woman is in a mad scramble to ape anything that is new and foreign.
    (A) With   (B) Because of
    (C) Instead of   (D) She is

18. _____ that contain both uranium and lead, scientists have been able to discover that Earth is at least 4 1/2 billion years old.
    (A) The study of rocks   (B) By studying rocks
    (C) It is the study of rocks   (D) They study rocks

19. The traditional material for making furniture is timber, _____, which is renewable.
    (A) dislike oil   (B) it is not like
    (C) not like oil   (D) unlike oil

20. _____ easier to pedal hills, the bicyclist shifts gears.

    (A) It was made   (B) To make it

    (C) Made it   (D) Rather than make it

21. By studying a living descendant of a supposedly extinct fish, scientists may learn many things about life _____ it existed millions of years ago.

    (A) as   (B) while

    (C) when   (D) because of

22. The inner bark of the breadfruit, _____ looks like mahogany and is used to make furniture and to build canoes.

    (A) when seasoned, it   (B) when it is seasoned

    (C) while is it seasoned   (D) because seasoning

23. North Europeans assumed that the tomato had poisonous properties _____ its relationship to deadly night shade.

    (A) for it had   (B) since that

    (C) because of   (D) in that

24. _____ such psychological rewards as relief from stress, deep relaxation can strengthen the immune system.

    (A) To yield   (B) Seeing that its yielding

    (C) In addition to yielding   (D) Nevertheless yields

25. _____ recently, California sequoia were thought to be the oldest living things on Earth.

(A) At   (B) Until

(C) Although it is   (D) Because of

26. _____ that simple method of a pendulum was first used to control the speed of a clock.

(A) Not until about 300 years ago

(B) It was not until about 300 years ago

(C) Until about 300 years ago

(D) About 300 years ago

27. Not until the early 1800's, when the value of field corn as grain and livestock feeding was recognized, _____.

(A) increasing acreage began

(B) its acreage began to increase

(C) did its acreage begin to increase

(D) with the beginning of increased acreage

28. _____ there is strict enforcement of the laws made by the government against golf courses taking water from public water way, little is about to change.

(A) Whenever   (B) Until

(C) Only   (D) Seeing that

29. Canadian women did not have the legal rights to vote _____ Nellie McClug strugged relentlessly in the early 20th century for them.

(A) when
(B) in that
(C) since
(D) until

30. _____ we travel, we try eating the local foods.

(A) Wherever
(B) And
(C) That
(D) At

31. _____ in Spain, merino sheep are now at home in many parts of the world.

(A) The originally breed
(B) Originally bred
(C) It is bred originally
(D) To breed originally

32. No matter how _____, much of the traditional handicrafts, architecture and just plain old ways of living have been swept away in the rush to industrialize.

(A) the Taiwanese have tried hard
(B) hard the Taiwanese have tried
(C) hardly have the Taiwanese tried
(D) have the Taiwanese tried

33. Pioneers liked to settle _____ there was plenty of wild game for food.

(A) and
(B) but
(C) however
(D) wherever

II、請找出文法錯誤之處，且寫出正確答案

34. <u>Despite of</u> some dangers, skin diving <u>has become</u> <u>a</u> popular form of
      A   B   C

   <u>recreation</u> in Taiwan.
     D

35. <u>Thank to</u> its extensive <u>and varied</u> corals, Pulau Redeng, Malaysia, was
      A   B

   once slated <u>for gazetting</u> as a marine park <u>but</u> now has been turned
                C   D

   into a golf resort.

36. One of the most harmful of all the snakes <u>found</u> in the U.S.A. is the
                                          A

   rattle snake, so called, <u>because</u> a curious set <u>of rattles</u> on <u>its</u> tail.
                          B   C   D

37. <u>Found</u> 16 years after the Pilgrims <u>landed at</u> Plymouth, Harvard
     A   B

   University was established by <u>a vote</u> of the great and general Court of
                              C

   <u>the</u> Massachusetts Bay Colony.
   D

38. Although it will take <u>as long as</u> years to grow a tree suitable <u>for harvesting</u>,
                              A   B

    <u>but</u> new trees are grown to replace <u>those which</u> have been cut.
     C   D

39. Magellan, <u>a</u> sixtheen-century Portuguese navigator, <u>sailed west</u> to
                 A   B

    reach the East Indies, thereby <u>proved</u> that <u>the earth</u> was round.
                                      C   D

40. <u>Because</u> <u>his proof</u> of the germ theory of disease, Doctor Pasteur
      A   B

    <u>revolutionized</u> <u>the practice</u> of medicine.
        C   D

第九章

形容詞子句

>>> EXERCISE 9

作為名詞（主詞、受詞與補語）的後置修飾語。形容詞子句中必有一個名詞，人、事或物與其所修飾的名詞有關聯，故又稱作關係子句。

目的在明確地界定名詞定義的範圍。

・God helps those (people) who help themselves.

・Men who (that) are predators destroy one another.

・Men, who are predators, destroy one another.

1. 關係代名詞：連接詞兼子句之代主詞或代受詞。

   (1) 先行詞為子句之主詞

      ・Anyone who (that) has information of my lost child will receive a reward.

      ・I don't like the stories which (that) have unhappy endings.

   (2) 先行詞為子句之受詞

      ・The man (whom/who/that) I wanted to see was away on holiday.

      ・Have you found the keys (which/that) you lost?

   (3) 先行詞為子句之所有格

      ・A window is a woman whose husband is dead.

      ・The house whose walls are made of glass is vulnerable.

        = The house with walls (made) of glass is vulnerable.

   (4) 先行詞子句中介系詞（in, at, about, with...）的受詞

      ・Do you know the girl with whom Tom is falling in love?

      ・The bed in which I slept last night is uncomfortable.

2. 關係副詞（why, where, when, that）：只作附加語之用，不可代主詞或受詞。

- The hotel where we stayed last night wasn't clean.
- The reason why we haven't got a car is that we can't afford one.
- Susan Warmer was born in an era, when the public taste favored the sentimentalism.

>>> III、形容詞子句、分詞片語與介系詞片語

- The woman who wears a red skirt was my dancing teacher.
  = The woman wearing a red skirt was my dancing teacher.
  = The woman in a red skirt was my dancing teacher.
- Inheritance laws which govern the distribution of property are complicated.
  = Inheritance laws governing the distribution of property are complicated.

{ 注意 } 序數、最高級之形容詞之後，或表目的、有未來含意的形容詞子句，須用不定詞片語

(to +V, to be +Ven) 作後置修飾。

- Jane M. Byrne was the first woman to be (who was) elected Mayor of Chicago.
- The case to be investigated (which will be investigated) will be reviewed tomorrow.

>>> **Exercise 9**

1. Paleontologists are scientists _____ studying prehistoric life through the study of fossils.
   (A) themselves to engage in
   (B) being engaged in
   (C) they are engaged in
   (D) who are engaged in

2. Through the lens of a telescope, people discovered the farthest stars in the solar system, which _____ to the naked eye.
   (A) invisible
   (B) the invisibility
   (C) are invisible
   (D) are the invisibility

3. Not every person who is indicted _____.
   (A) of guilt
   (B) is guilty
   (C) to be guilty
   (D) guilty

4. The centipede's long body is divided into two parts, _____ has one pair of legs.
   (A) which
   (B) each
   (C) each of which
   (D) that

5. The ideal of Mahayana is that those _____ have achieved "enlightment" should return to the earthly realm to teach and help people who are still suffered.
   (A) people
   (B) which
   (C) who
   (D) they

6. After the bananas have been collected, the stalks _____ are cut down.
   (A) on which they grow   (B) which they grow
   (C) growing on which they   (D) they grow on them

7. A college education should provide the background _____ each person can develop his own values and ideas.
   (A) when   (B) which
   (C) only when   (D) from which

8. Polo is a game _____ players ride horses and use long-handled wood hammers to hit a ball in an attempt to score goals.
   (A)when   (B)which
   (C) is when   (D) in which

9. Greenwich, England, offers the world standard of time, _____ set their watches and clocks.
   (A) which people   (B) by which people
   (C) people   (D) which do people

10. In skin diving, divers often seem suspended in a world of water _____ _____ neither the surface above nor the bottom below can be seen.
    (A) where was   (B) it was where
    (C) where was it   (D) where

11. Balloons cannot provide reliable transportation because they must go
    _____ blow them.
    (A) do where the winds   (B) where the winds
    (C) when the winds   (D) do when the winds

12. Sea anemones are almost stationary and can move very slowly over
    the surfaces _____ .
    (A) to which they are attached (B) attached them
    (C) which they are attached   (D) where are they attached

13. In 17 century AD, Buddhism was carried to Tibet, _____ the sky
    was bluer than anywhere else on earth, and the new religion took root.
    (A) when   (B) that
    (C) which   (D) where

14. Once a student registers, official records "folders" are transferred from
    the Admission Office to the Registration Office, _____ until the
    student graduates.
    (A) where are they held   (B) which is held
    (C) which they are held   (D) where they are held

15. Geologists believed that the Berlins land bridge disappeared about
    14,000 years ago and massive glaciers melted, _____ caused the
    sea level to rise several hundred feet worldwide.
    (A) it   (B) which
    (C) which it   (D) thus

16. Each cell contains a number of chromosomes, _____ genes determining what characteristics the animal or plant will have.

(A) each has
(B) with each
(C) has each
(D) each with

17. Many of the trees native to Taiwan yield useful woods, _____ of high market value.

(A) which is
(B) a number of which are
(C) each has
(D) they are all

18. The revolution in South Africa is a transfer of power, _____ maintains the management skills of the minority regime with the support of the majority.

(A) which
(B) that
(C) by which
(D) what

19. Football and baseball _____ currently played in the United States are basic modifications of games that originated in England

(A) that
(B) are
(C) as
(D) which are

20. Anthropologists _____ the origins of people have found bones and wall drawings to increase their knowledge of early human history.

(A) studying
(B) who they study
(C) study
(D) have studied

21. A majority of people in the United States can get the protein their bodies _____ from the food they eat.
    (A) requires   (B) require
    (C) to require   (D) requiring

22. The moon contains all the elements found on earth, including _____.
    (A) elements for generating of nuclear energy
    (B) those are required for generating nuclear energy
    (C) they that are necessary for the generation of nuclear energy
    (D) those required to generate nuclear energy

23. In the cells of living systems, there are many delicate transitions, _____ _____ one compound is changed into another.
    (A) when   (B) in which
    (C) is when   (D) which

24. They create a series of forums _____ issues of education can be discussed in ways that will have a national impact.
    (A) which   (B) where
    (C) when   (D) how

25. Flag Staff, one of the USA's west coast scenic wonders, is a captivating base _____ people can explore Arizona's Grand Canyon and Painted Desert.
    (A) how   (B) which
    (C) where   (D) so that

26. There are a number of financial aid programs, available especially for students of color, _____ they are intended to encourage to enter doctoral study.
   (A) whom   (B) that
   (C) which   (D) in which

27. The centipedes have poisonous claws, _____ just behind the head, are dangerous.
   (A) which are located   (B) located
   (C) which locating   (D) which, located

28. Education is a science _____ educators use a rigorous set of methods and techniques to document observation that can be checked by others.
   (A) in that   (B) that is
   (C) which   (D) whereas

29. Among the most precious stones, diamond is the hardest, long-lasting substance _____.
   (A) science to know   (B) knowing science
   (C) science is known   (D) known to science

30. Democracy advocates individualism, _____ the individual's freedom and self expression.
   (A) who preserves   (B) the preservation
   (C) it is preserved   (D) preserving

II、請找出文法錯誤之處，且寫出正確答案

31. Life on earth is <u>based on</u> photosynthesis <u>which</u> the energy radiated by
                      A   B
    the sun is <u>converted to drive</u> the metabolic process of <u>living</u> organisms.
                      C   D

32. Charlies Chaplin was <u>the greatest star</u> of silent films, <u>which</u> inspiration
                              A   B
    gave hope and <u>laughter</u> to <u>the world</u>.
                      C   D

33. <u>Thanks to</u> the world's donation <u>to famine relief</u> in Ethiopia, a few million
        A   B
    <u>which</u> would otherwise be dead <u>are alive</u> and beginning to hope again.
        C   D

34. A desert is a land <u>where</u> plants, animals, and people cannot get all the
                          A
    water they <u>in need</u> because the climate is <u>either</u> too dry or <u>too cold</u>.
                  B   C   D

35. Harassment can create <u>an</u> environment <u>which</u> access <u>to education</u> and
                              A   B   C
    employment is <u>diminished</u>.
                      D

104   英語文法與修辭

36. A hurricane is a huge circle of wind which it forms around the trade
                        A   B   C
    winds in the Atlantic.
              D

37. Students who drops below half time for any reason should be aware
              A   B
    that such changes will have an immediate impact on their loan.
              C   D

38. This college has an excellent faculty, which are committed to the
                      A   B   C
    advancement of knowledge and to the improvement of practice.
                                              D

39. Every thing on earth is made up of atoms or molecules, which is take
                          A   B   C
    part in chemical reactions.
        D

40. It is a decent custom by which prescribes that we shall say nothing but
                          A   B   C
    good about the dead.
              D

名詞子句

>>> EXERCISE 10

```
結 ┬ 限定 ┬ That 子句─That he's passed the test is certainly true.
  │      └ Wh- 子句─Whether he is alive or not is still a question.
  │                  Can you tell me how I can reach him?
  │                  What I want to know is your decision.
構 └ 非限定 ┬ 不定詞（To-V）─To be a member is to be among the elite.
           └ 動名詞（V-ing）─Falling in love is a wonderful experience.
```

{注意} 非限定名詞子句乃是限定名詞子句依經濟原則的衍化而成
　　　 的。例如：

‧I don't know whom I could depend on.（限定）

　=I don't know whom to depend on.（非限定）

‧We decided that we would adopt the poor child.

　= We decided to adopt the poor child.

>>> **Ⅰ、功能**

1. 當主詞

主詞	述詞
‧ That the evolution within the algae began very early	is evident.
‧ Whether or not we would go on a picnic	was still a question.
‧ To give up the job	would be foolish.
‧ Wearing so short a skirt	is quite inconvenient.
‧ What he has done	frightened me.

(1) 名詞子句當主詞常轉換成 It...that 或 It...to 句型。

(2) 動名詞子句，必須改成 to V：

　　‧ It is quite inconvenient to wear so short a skirt.

(3) what 名詞子句後移，必須引進介系詞：

．It frightened me ＿＿＿ what he has done.

2. 當受詞

   (1) 及物動詞之受詞

主詞 + 及物動詞	受詞
They whole family decided	(that) they would immigrate.
I can't believe	what I just heard.
He claimed himself	to be expert of crime.
We hate	causing you any trouble.

   (2) 介系詞受詞（that -, to +V 子句除外）

主詞 + 不及物動詞	Prep	受詞
No one was consulted	about	who should be on the committee.
I am tried	of	being treated as a child.
We were surprised	at	John's making this mistake.

{注意} what 可代替名詞子句中的主詞或受詞：Footnotes often cite the source of authority for what the author says.

3. 當補語

   (1) 主詞補語

主詞	動詞	主詞補語
What the kids need	is	that their parents concern.
What I said	is	what I meant.
The question	is	whether I should accept his offer.
My purpose	is	to get through the challenge.
Seeing	is	believing.

(2) 受詞補語

主詞 + 受詞	受詞	受詞補語
I saw	John	where he shouldn't be.
He denied	the rumor	that he has been arrested.
I gave	my wife	whatever she wanted.

(3) 形容詞補語

主詞	形容詞	形容詞補語
We were	convinced	that he was suitable for the job.
I am not	sure	when he will return.
I am	glad	to work with you.
Kids are	happy	playing computer games.

>>> II、名詞子句與形容詞 that 子句之區別

· He denied the rumor that there would be a General Election this year.

(He denied the rumor that was reported by the BBC news.)

· The question whether he will win a seat in this-year legislative election is going to be announced.

(Dr. Lee gave the answers to the question that was presented by David.)

>>> III、同位語（**Oppositive**）

1. 確認：An extremely popular major, A1 Jackson was able to redirect the city's priorities.
2. 命名：The new invention, Bubble Jet Printer, seemed quite useful.
3. 指派：John Harvard, the founder of Harvard University, had a very keen interest in theology at a very young age.
4. 同義：The lift, or elevator, is an antique.
5. 舉例：We traveled several European cities, such as Rome, Athen, Paris.
6. 關係全句（Sentential relative clause）：
   ・It was raining hard, which kept me indoors.
   ・She couldn't come to the party, which was pity.

>>> **Exercise 10**

1. At the end of the decade, the UN had reported that the gap between the rich and the poor had widened and that _____ for many of the poor countries is a region of famine and revolution.
    (A) what lies ahead   (B) lies ahead
    (C) it lies ahead   (D) was lain ahead

2. The fact _____ the Universal Declaration of Rights has been accepted all over the world has improved our control over the way people, under all kinds of leadership, are treated.
    (A) of   (B) that
    (C) which   (D) is that

3. _____ from the airplane wreck was a miracle.
    (A) The child could survive   (B) Why the child could survive
    (C) That the child could survive (D) When the child could survive

4. It is recently proved_____ the laser can be used toperform bloodless, painless surgery.
    (A) where   (B) until
    (C) while   (D) that

5. Footnotes of ten cite the source of authority for _____.
    (A) what does the author say   (B) what the author says
    (C) that the author has said   (D) the author says

6. _____ the scientists fear is the continued use of fossil fuels and the destruction of forest which will increase the quantity of carbon dioxide in the atmosphere.
   (A) What   (B) How
   (C) That   (D) Both

7. We know little about _____ primitive people came to use money.
   (A) which   (B) what
   (C) how   (D) whether

8. Feelings are _____ makes for humanity.
   (A) that   (B) those
   (C) which   (D) what

9. The theory _____ human beings were related to apes challenged the religious views of how life on earth came about.
   (A) which   (B) in which
   (C) that   (D) because

10. Mass determines _____ a star, often passing through the red giant stage, will compress itself into a white dwarf, a neutron star or a black hole.
    (A) what   (B) that
    (C) whether   (D) why

11. As you read, try to relate new reading material to _____.

    (A) that you have already known

    (B) you have already known

    (C) the knowing of your

    (D) what you have already known

12. To describe a woman as having a nice personality may imply _____.

    (A) She is unattractive physically

    (B) that she is physically unattractive

    (C) is that she is physically unattractive

    (D) the physical unattractive of her

13. To verify _____ adequate financial arrangement has been made, students are required to submit a letter from a U.S. bank.

    (A) which   (B) what

    (C) since   (D) that

14. Therapists _____ treatment of those who seek help to quit smoking or overeating is rarely successful.

    (A) find that   (B) finding that

    (C) are found   (D) to find

15. Lucy Terry, once a slave in Massachusetts, was one of the few black women to leave record of _____ in the American life.

    (A) that life was alike   (B) what was like

    (C) life was like   (D) which is life like

16. The academic interest in perception mostly comes from questions about the sources and validity of what _____.
    (A) it is known as human knowledge
    (B) is known as human knowledge
    (C) known as human knowledge
    (D) is human knowledge knowing

17. The person submitting the complaint must include a detailed description of _____ and why it should be considered a violation of another's rights.
    (A) what occurred   (B) it occurred
    (C) something occurred   (D) which was occurred

18. We are consciously aware of _____ should golf course construction go unchecked.
    (A) it could be at stake   (B) why being at stake
    (C) that could be at stake (D) what could be at stake

19. Because he had been alone at that time, none of his family were aware _____ has occurred during their absence.
    (A) which that   (B) of that
    (C) that which   (D) of what

20. No one is completely sure _____ purpose people made and carved six huge and mysterious stone statues of Easter Island.
    (A) how   (B) whom
    (C) what   (D) that

21. Bitter arguments and debates between the churches and the public raged back and forth over rival views of _____ life on earth came about.

(A) that
(B) which
(C) whether
(D) how

22. Briefly speaking, a theory is an abstract symbolic representation of _____ reality.

(A) what it is considered
(B) that is considered
(C) what is considered
(D) how is it considered

23. Charles Darwin's "The Origin of Species" set out the revolutionary view _____ all living things, from ants to elephants, had evolved by natural selection.

(A) which
(B) that
(C) what
(D) if

24. _____ that laws have been passed to assure women equal access to educational and employment opportunities.

(A) There is certain
(B) Certainly
(C) To certain
(D) It is certain

25. Sugar converts anaerobically into carbon dioxid and alcohol through yeasts' fermentation, _____.

(A) a chemical reaction induced by living ferments
(B) a chemical reaction is induced by living ferments
(C) which it is a chemical reaction living ferments induce
(D) that is a chemical reaction induced by living ferments

26. A synthetic radioactive metallic element, _____, an Italian-born American atomic and nuclear physicist.
    (A) it was named for Enrico Fermi
    (B) Enrico Fermi named it
    (C) which is named for Enrico Fermi
    (D) Fermium was named for Enrico Fermi

27. Maria Tallchief _____, whose best performance was the Fire Bird, a beautiful wild bird with magic power.
    (A) she was an Osage Native American dancer
    (B) an Osage Native American dancer
    (C) was an Osage Native American dancer
    (D) to be an Osage Native American dancer

28. Harvard University, _____ higher education, has a long tradition of leadership in the academic world.
    (A) the oldest institution of
    (B) was the oldest institution of
    (C) the school was the oldest institution of
    (D) the oldest institution being

29. _____, who worked extensively to supporting blac communities to against racism, getting better salaries for teaching and ending the employment of children in factories.
    (A) The Universal Declaration on Human Rights of Eleanor Roosevelt
    (B) Eleanor Roosevelt's the Universal Declaration Human Rights
    (C) The Universal Declaration of Human Rights was championed by Eleanor Roosevelt
    (D) Eleanor Roosevelt championed the Universal Declaration of Human Rights

30. The bacteriologist, _____, has saved million of lives.
    (A) who is Alexander Fleming discovering penicillin
    (B) Alexander Fleming discovered penicillin
    (C) discovering Penicillin of the bacteriologist
    (D) Alexander Fleming who discovered penicillin

31. George Hegel was born in Stuttgat, Germany, in 1770, _____as Beethoven.
    (A) was the same year
    (B) it was the same year
    (C) the same year
    (D) of the same year

32. John Dewey, _____ believed that thinking is the instrument for solving problems and knowledge is tied to a practical solution.
    (A) was a pragmatist   (B) a pragmatist
    (C) who, a pragmatist   (D) who was a pragmatist, he

33. _____, the builder of the Louvre.
    (A) Perrault was a typical architect of the baroque style
    (B) A typical architect of the baroque style is Perrault
    (C) A typical architect of the baroque style being Perrault
    (D) Perrault's baroque style architecture

34. _____, impressionism was first used by a journalist in 1874 to ridicule Claude Monet's painting "Impression" _____ Sunrise.

(A) One of the 19th century's movements

(B) That one of the 19th century's movements

(C) It was one of the 19th century's movements

(D) One of the 19th century's movements was

II、請找出文法錯誤之處，且寫出正確答案

35. Hurricane sometimes sucks up a great mound of water and sends it
                                              A

thundering ahead to destroy which lies in its path.
            B   C   D

36. Recently, there has been considerable debate over that increased taxes
                        A   B

should be a first or last resort in balancing the government budget.
            C   D

37. So called critical intelligence is values are tied to human desire and
                                    A

its satisfaction and human mind will help us see the consequences of
    B   C

any desire, thus leading us to a satisfactory solution.
            D

38. There is a great gap in which is known about beauty in art-should an
         A   B

    artist seek to create beauty or simply to express itself.
                       C   D

39. That copper and bronze were first used in Asia is an interesting
      A   B   C
    question in science history.
                 D

40. There would be a fairly long speech in a play is often presented as
         A   B   C
    a recitative in an opera.
      D

第十一章

# 比較結構
>>> EXERCISE 11

>>> I、功能

藉著形容詞與副詞的字形變化來表示兩個人、事、物比較的程度。

>>> II、字形變化

形容詞或副詞的字形變化,依其音節來變化。

1. 單音節

形容詞 + er/ + est			副詞 + er/ + est		
原級	比較級	最高級	原級	比較級	最高級
young	younger	youngest	fast	faster	fastest
thin	thinner	thinnest	soon	sooner	soonest

{注意} 有些形容詞如 strange, tired, real,因字母組合或發音上的
考量,須採 more, the most 的形式。

2. 雙音節
   (1) 一般雙音節的形容詞或副詞皆採 -er, -est: pretty, early, busy...。
   (2) 字尾是 -ful, -less, -ed, -ing, -ous, -ive, -ous 的形容詞或 -ly
       結尾的副詞,採 more, the most: boring, slowly, confused,
       confused, creative, careful, likely, ...。

3. 三音節以上:凡是上含三個音節以上的形容詞,如 important,
   essential, responsible, wonderful...etc., 採 more, the more 皆可。

4. 不規則字形變化的形容詞與副詞

形容詞			副詞		
原級	比較級	最高級	原級	比較級	最高級
bad	worse	worst	badly	worse	worst
far	farther	farthest	far	further	furthest
good	better	best	well	better	best
little	less	least			
late	latter	last	late	later	latest
many/much	more	most			

5. 有些形容詞本身的意義是絕對的，無法做相對性的比較，因此
   沒有比較級或最高級，這些字包括：unique、perfect、single、
   round、square。

>>> **III、句型與用法**

1. 同等級

比較對象	動詞	Adv.	形容／副詞	conj.	被比較對象
1. She	is	as	charming	as	I ever knew.
2. The city	isn't	so	crowded	as	it usually was.
3. I	drives	as	carefully	as	he (does).
4. Jim	runs	as	fast	as	he used to.

2. 比較級

比較對象	動詞（受詞）	形容／副詞 + er	連接詞	被比較對象
Ann	works	harder	than	he (does).
He	speaks	more fluently	than	(do) I.
John	knows food	better	than	Jane knows wine.

(1) 同樣事物才能比較：My car is more expensive than you.

(2) 避免雙重比較的錯誤：She is more taller than her brother.

(3) 隱含比較：有時候，把現有的狀況與過去的狀況做比較，有特定的時間副詞加以暗示。

  ‧ The cost of living in Taipei has been rising higher each year.

(4) 慣用語：the higher education, the lower/higher lip, the upper/lower jaw.

(5) 拉丁語系：本身已有比較的意味，不須加 er 或 more, 以 to 代替 than。

  ‧ He is (far) superior to me in English writing.

  ‧ My speech is (far) inferior to his.

(6) 強化副詞：突顯形容／副詞修飾的程度。一般 very 強化原級的形容詞或副詞，much 強化比較級的形容詞或副詞，拉丁語系的字以 far 來強化。

  ‧ Very good, much better (= far better)

  ‧ very interesting, much more interesting（有趣多了）

3. 最高級

		補語 / 副詞	
Christ	is	the tallest girl	in her class.
Einstein	was	the greatest (Scientist)	of all scientists.
It	is	the least interesting story	that I've ever heard.
James	speaks	best	in the contest.

{注意} 兩者間的比較也有需要 the 的時候：She is the taller (one) of the twins.

4. 雙層比較結構（the more..., the more...）

【the more + adj/adv + S +V..., the more adj/adv + S + V...】

・the longer I wanted, the more impatient I became.

・The more expensive the hotel (is), the better the service (is).（be 動詞常被省略。）

{注意} 兩個子句之間有因果關係，前者爲「因」（副詞子句），後者爲「果」（主要子句），兩者的次序不可顛倒。如把主要的子句挪前，則主句必須恢復正常次順，去掉逗點與定冠詞 the。

・When you drive faster, you will feel better.

= The faster you drive（因）the better you feel.（果）

= You fell better the faster you drive.

>>> Exercise 11

1. The more equipment a teacher needs, _____.
   (A) which the activities become less accessible
   (B) and the less accessible activities become
   (C) the less accessible the activities become
   (D) activities become less accessible

2. The coarser the sediment, _____.
   (A) where the beach is steeper and narrower
   (B) and the steeper and narrower the beach
   (C) the beach is steeper and narrow
   (D) the steeper and narrower the beach

3. The stronger_____ magnetic field, the greater the voltage produced by a generator.
   (A) than the   (B) is the
   (C) that the   (D) the

4. The higher the standard of living and the greater the national wealth, the _____.
   (A) greater is the amount of paper is used
   (B) greater amount of paper is used
   (C) amount of paper is used is greater
   (D) greater the amount of paper used

5. Grand Canyon itself defies human comprehension. The more you know about it, _____.
   (A) the more awesome it becomes
   (B) it becomes more awesome
   (C) than it becomes awesome
   (D) and more awesome it become

6. The better the initial understanding of the reading, _____ to integrate information.
   (A) the easier will be   (B) it will be easier
   (C) so it will be the easier (D) the easier it will be

7. The higher the per capital income and the greater he national wealth, the _____.
   (A) more are the opportunities offered
   (B) opportunities are offered more
   (C) more opportunities are offered
   (D) more the opportunities offered

8. The greater an object's mass, the more difficult it is _____.
   (A) to speed it up or slow it down
   (B) it speeds up or slows down
   (C) than speeding it up or slowing it down
   (D) than speeding up or slowing down

9. The more arid the continent, the less the amount of annual precipitation _____ .
   (A) runs off that
   (B) runs it off
   (C) that runs it off
   (D) that runs off

10. The damage to heart tissue grows _____ .
   (A) worse the more the exposure to tobacco smoke increases
   (B) the worse, the more exposure to tobacco smoke increases
   (C) worse than the exposure to tobacco smoke increases more
   (D) worse than it, the more the exposure to tobacco smoke increases

11. A body weighs_____ from the surface of the Earth.
   (A) less the farther it gets
   (B) the farther it gets, the less
   (C) less than it gets farther
   (D) less than it, the father it gets

12. The annual worth of Utah's manufacturing is greater than _____ .
   (A) that of its mining and farming combined
   (B) mining and farming combination
   (C) that mining and farming combined
   (D) of its combination mining and farming

13. The American judicial system provides more safeguards for accused persons_____ country.
   (A) than does that of any other
   (B) does than the other
   (C) than does any other
   (D) than any other does that

14. Some surveys indicate that proposals incorporating with graphics stand 20 percent more likelihood of being approved than _____.
    (A) those do without graphics (B) which have no graphics
    (C) do those without graphics (D) that does without graphics

15. The ratio of managers' salaries to _____ substantially lower in Taiwan than in the United States.
    (A) ordinary workers is (B) those of ordinary workers is
    (C) ordinary workers' are (D) that of ordinary workers is

16. Small as it is in comparison with other stars, the sun fires out 2 billion times more heat & light than _____.
    (A) the earth absorbs (B) the earth to absorb
    (C) the earth which absorbs (D) absorbed by the earth

17. Eastern Taiwan generally receives more rain than _____ western Taiwan.
    (A) does (B) in
    (C) it does in (D) in it does

18. Emphasis is placed upon conceptual understanding, problem-solving and critical thinking _____ rote memorization.
    (A) instead (B) rather than
    (C) in addition to (D) as well

19. The effects of the bipartisan committee were marked as much by frustration_____ success.

    (A) as it was by   (B) as by

    (C) as there was   (D) as well

II、請找出文法錯誤之處，且寫出正確答案

20. <u>Light</u> travels <u>more faster</u> than anything else <u>that</u> has ever been

    A   B   C

<u>measured</u>.

   D

21. Sane historians <u>have argued</u> that science <u>moves forward</u> not so much

                  A   B

because of the insights of great thinkers <u>but</u> because of <u>more</u> mundane

                                      C   D

development.

22. It's necessary for people <u>to learn</u> how to drive <u>their</u> cars with <u>such</u>

                            A   B   C

<u>little chance</u> of accident as possible.

     D

23. <u>The use</u> of chemical insecticide <u>in</u> this country <u>is as</u> extensive than ten

    A   B   C

years <u>ago</u>.

    D

24. The energy <u>expended</u> <u>per unit</u> of production in Japan is twice as much

           A   B

   as <u>it</u> of Taiwan's <u>expenditure</u>.

      C   D

25. Arguments <u>against using</u> children as courtroom witness are <u>that</u>

              A   B

   children's memories are more malleable and <u>less trust-worthy</u> than <u>adults</u>.

                                   C   D

26. After <u>seeing a terror movie</u>, women are much <u>susceptible</u> <u>than men</u>.

       A   B   C   D

27. In an accident <u>with an automobile</u>, a bicycle <u>being</u> <u>the light</u> vehicle, is

                    A   B   C

   likely to come out <u>second best</u>.

                D

28. Stanford University, <u>famous as</u> one of Northern California's several

                    A

   institutions of <u>high education</u> <u>is</u> sometimes called " the Harvard of

                  B   C

  <u>the West</u>".

    D

29. One of the plants <u>covering</u> the Earth's surface many <u>thousands</u> of
                              A   B

    years ago <u>far common</u> <u>than now</u> was the fern.
                    C   D

30. <u>Decaying matter</u> on the forest floor is a <u>far great</u> source of the acidity
           A   B

    in mountain lakes than <u>is</u> the acid rain that <u>falls on</u> these lakes.
                              C   D

31. In the 19th century, artists were <u>first</u> interested in political <u>and social</u>
                                     A   B

    causes, and <u>latter</u> in the problems <u>of painting</u>.
                  C   D

32. It seems that modern customers are <u>more interested</u> in the way things
    A   B

    appear than in the way <u>they</u> <u>are</u> actually.
                           C   D

33. Sri Lanka is <u>not so</u> large <u>in size</u> as Ireland, but its population exceeds
                       A   B

    <u>Ireland</u> by <u>several million</u> people.
      C   D

34. Among the many strange fish that inhabit the waters near the bottom
      A   B   C

    of the ocean, one of the more unusual is the torpedo fish.
                                D

35. As a nationally known educational reformer, Gardner considers that
             A

    the present effort is "much more rooted" in the real world than did
         B   C   D

    traditional methods.

36. The five hundred largest manufacturing firms in the USA produce
             A

    goods worth almost as much as those of the remaining four hundred
                    B   C   D

    thousand firms.

37. The Taiwanese are eating more than twice meat per person as they did
         A   B   C   D
    in 1950.

38. He chose abstract math because it is less likely to be associated with
                                     A   B

    past experience as are other subjects.
                 C   D

39. Laser beams have <u>the most unique</u> ability <u>to perform</u> bloodless,
                              A   B

   <u>painless</u> <u>surgery</u>.
       C   D

40. <u>It's thought</u> that Pakua ceiling is <u>the distinctivest feature</u> to Taiwan
           A   B

   temples and <u>the one</u> in Lungshan temple is the oldest and <u>most peculiar</u>.
                    C   D

第十二章

倒裝句

>>> EXERCISE 12

句子中的主詞和其運作語（operator）互相調換位置。運作語指助動詞、do、或 be 動詞。

- Never did I make you down and out.
- Here is your work permit.

有下列各種情況會採倒裝句

>>> I、Yes-no 問句、Wh- 問句

He does not accept your suggestion. → Does he accept your suggestion?

What did you find in your investigation?

>>> II、追問句（Tag-question）

You checked out the book, didn't you?

You are a professional football player. aren't you?

>>> III、感嘆句

強調副詞的意涵時，把副詞到片語或句子之前。

1. 副詞 + 主詞（代名詞）+ 動詞
   - Up he jumped. (= He jumped up.)
   - Away they flew. (= They flew away.)
2. 副詞 + 動詞 + 主詞（一般名詞）
   - Along the rocky New England coast are small areas of sand and gravel beach.
   - On the hill stands my house. (= My house stands on the hill.)
   - Here come his parents!

否定、部分否定或少量的字置於字首時，句子須倒裝。

· Never had I heard such a big lie. (= I had never heard such a big lie.)
· Not only didn't he mail the letter but also he forgot to pick up the laundry.
· No sooner had he arrived home than he planned to start another journey.
· Not a penny will I lend you.
· Only in this way can we improve our financial situation.
· Not until a baby is six-month old, does it begin the initial stages of language development.
· Rarely did he watch midnight TV programs.
· By no means shall I invest in the stock market.
· Flying demands greater skill than does driving.

>>> **V、特殊字組**

1. So/Such...that
· So peculiar were his ways that no one likes to work with him.
原句：His ways were so peculiar that no one likes to work with.
強調「peculiar」（怪異）則 So peculiar 至於句首，主、動詞需倒裝。

2. so/nor/neither
· His shoes are brightly polished and so is his briefcase.
原句：His shoes are brightly polished. His briefcase is brightly polished, too.
兩句合併，用 and so 銜接，強調主詞「His briefcase」，因英文句子最重要的關鍵字在句尾。故「His briefcase」置句尾，採倒裝型態。

- I couldn't understand a word they said nor could they understand me!（nor 本身是連接詞，故不需用 and 銜接）

3. among which

- There are several types of alternatives to fossil fuels, among which may be most mentioned solar energy.

原句：There are several types of alternatives to <u>fossil fuels</u>.

Solar energy may be most mentioned among those <u>fossil fuels</u>.

兩個句子組成一句，後句為形容詞子句，相關字以 among which 為了強調「solar energy」故置於句尾，採倒裝句型。

>>> Exercise 12

1. Not until the arrival of the atomic age _____ fully known.
   (A) that the value of uranium was
   (B) was the value of uranium
   (C) when uranium's value was
   (D) the value of uranium was

2. _____ have the inspectors finished their investigation.
   (A) Since that   (B) Although
   (C) By no means   (D) Not only

3. Only when female eels have reached the ocean region where they were born _____ they lay eggs.
   (A) had   (B) are
   (C) do   (D) that

4. _____ all money due from prior term bills is paid in fall will students be permitted to register in any term.
   (A) Never   (B) Until
   (C) Not until   (D) After

5. Laser has a number of applications _____ may be most mentioned its use in medical surgical operation.
   (A) among which   (B) which
   (C) and which   (D) each of which

6. _____ exerted by typhoons that it has been known to lift railroads off their tracks.

   (A) The great force is   (B) The force is such great

   (C) How great the force is   (D) So great is the force

7. _____ at mixing strength and sensitivity she gave to the female characters that she became one of the excellent American playwrights.

   (A) So successful, Lillian Hellman

   (B) So successful was Lillian Hellman

   (C) Lillian Hellman so successful

   (D) Because Lillian Hellman so successful

II、請找出文法錯誤之處，且寫出正確答案

8. Only in the last 100 years large areas of tropical jungles been cleaned

             A   B   C

   for banana plantations.

             D

9. Few colleges are able to provide parking facilities for students, nor do

   A   B   C

   students allowed to park their car on university premises.

                                    D

10. Along the Amazon River's shores are the world's largest forest, in which

    A   B   C   D

   varied and abundant foliage grows.

11. Florida's travel industry is suffering <u>as a result</u> of a sluggish economy,

                                          A

   <u>a stretch of</u> bad weather <u>as good as</u> the chilling effects of persistent

         B   C

   <u>terrorist</u> activity.

        D

12. <u>Such does</u> the <u>nation-wide</u> appeal of recreation that tennis courts or

        A   B

   swimming pools are now one of <u>the key selling points</u> of holiday

                                            C

   resorts and <u>residential</u> development.

                D

13. <u>The basis</u> of Buddha teachings argued that only by accepting that our

     A

   existence is <u>bound up with</u> suffering and that this suffering is the

               B

   product of our own will and desire, <u>we can</u> escape from <u>the endless</u>

                                    C   D

   <u>cycle</u> of death and rebirth.

第十三章

介系詞

>>> EXERCISE 13

・依功能，介系詞可分類如下：

1. at + 特定的時刻
   ・at noon, at dawn, at the moment, at ten o'clock
2. on + 特定的日子
   ・on the Christmas, on the morning of Jun 6 on the wedding anniversary, on the holiday
3. in + 一段時期
   ・in January, in 1990/the 1990's, in summer
4. for + 特定時期之短
   ・for two years, for a long time, during the
5. during
   ・WWII, during my school days, during my vacation
6. from...to + 特定日子的起迄
   ・from 1988 to 1990, five to six

>>> **II、地點**

1. at + 特定的地點、場合、或較小的地方
   ・at home/school, at the university
   at a concert/conference, at football court
2. in + 較大的地方
   ・in the world, in Asia, in the Pacific Ocean,
   + 在…之內
   ・in the field, in the water, in bed, in the chair
3. on + 表面或周遭
   ・on the table, (at table), on...Road, on the sea

on the board, on my way home

4. to + 方向 / 傾向
  ・go to, point to, torn to pieces, rise to, turn to

5. for + 目的
  ・leave for, launch for

>>> III、因果 / 目的

for, because of, (result) from/in, (in order) to, despite

>>> IV、方法

by + Ving, with + a tool, by means of

>>> V、組成

(come) from, (be made up) of

>>> VI、相對關係

cheek to cheek, second to none, 5 point to 3.30 miles to the gallon.
the key to the this lock, answers/solutions to, the guide to

>>> VII、介系詞片語

a rise/an increase/a decrease/trouble	in
damage/an invitation/a reaction/contribute	to
connect/contact with, an advantage	of

>>> Exercise 13

請找出文法錯誤之處，且寫出正確答案

1. Prior 1914, Cubism and futurism were two related movements as seen
       A   B

   in the works of Archipenko/Picasso and Boccioni respectively.
       C   D

2. Darwin's research and his controversial book have been placed human
                           A   B

   beings to an overall pattern of revolution.
           C   D

3. From the beginning of the Christian period until the Renaissance of
             A   B

   the 15th century, philosophy concentrated almost exclusively on the
                                               C

   relation of faith and reason.
             D

4. At the 12th century, a cultural revolution took place and education
    A   B

   shifted from the liberal arts toward logic and science.
       C   D

5. Wild yaks, a wild ox <u>native of</u> Tibet, may be <u>found living</u> <u>at the height</u>
                                     A   B   C

of 500 meters <u>above</u> sea level.
                   D

6. Sri Lanka is an island <u>located in</u> the Indian Ocean <u>separated from</u>
                                  A   B

India by a channel only 35 Kilometers wide <u>with</u> <u>its</u> narrowest point.
                                                     C   D

7. When a hearing <u>on</u> Rights and Responsibility is <u>conducted</u>, the
                                 A   B

chairperson will be <u>responsible of</u> initiating, moderating <u>and ending</u>
                                  C   D

the hearing.

8. <u>Dislike</u> <u>those</u> of neighboring Pompeii, the inhabitants of Herculaneum
    A   B

had time <u>to flee</u> before their city was buried <u>under</u> volcanic mud of
                  C   D

Vesuvius.

9. The light of a firefly <u>comes of</u> a mineral called phosphorus, which <u>is</u>
                             A   B

found <u>in small amounts</u> in <u>its</u> body.
              C   D

10. In ancient times, the appearance of a comet aroused great alarm to people.
    A   B   C   D

11. The lobster has a small head with a pair of feelers, which substitute to
              A   B   C   D
    eyes.

12. Yearly, as mating time draws near, the penguins swim to their breeding
    A   B   C
    grounds and gather with huge flocks.
                          D

13. Among poisonous snakes, the rattle snake is, for far, the most common.
    A   B   C   D

14. High-grade iron ore mined in Sweden has resulted of the famous high-
        A   B   C   D
    quality Swedish steel.

15. Over and over, she tried hard to gain admission for a medical school.
    A   B   C   D

16. A troy pound used by jewelers is similar as a weight that was used by
    A   B   C   D
    druggists.

17. Meteors are hot celestial bodies entering the atmosphere of the Earth in
                 A   B   C   D

    great speeds.

18. The ruins of pharaoh Hatshepsut's funeral temple still stand to remind
      A   B   C

    us from a powerful unusual pharaoh.
                        D

19. Quick silver is the only metal that keeps its liquid form in normal
                  A   B   C   D

    temperatures.

20. Installment buying has become common in the USA and many
          A
    families furnish their homes by purchasing goods with credit.
             B   C   D

21. The bird hides its nest inside broad flat leaves by sewing together the
             A   B

    edges of the leaves at its needle-shaped beak.
              C   D

22. Mercury is the silver-white substance, which expands or contracts
                           A   B

    according upon changes in temperature.
           C   D

23. Many art patrons are far less experts in distinguishing authentic art
            A   B   C
    and fakes.
        D

24. International Students are generally restricted of working outside
                          A   B   C
    the campus.
        D

25. Professor Judah will focus this module into the math teaching with
                          A   B   C   D
    educational technologies.

26. Many educators believe that the key of improving the achievement of
                                          A
    low-income minority students was to improve their self-concept.
            B   C   D

27. The diet of a starfish is composed by clams, mussels, snails and other
        A   B   C   D
    small sea creatures.

28. The new constitution outlaws unfair discrimination at the basis of
                          A   B   C
    "race, gender, ethnic or social region, belief or color".

D

29. The judiciary is to be independent and impartial and subject only with
                    A   B   C
    the constitution and the law.
                            D

30. Nine provinces, each has its own legislature and premier, have the
                          A   B
    rights to adopt their own official languages.
              C   D

31. The skin keeps out water and dirt, assists on keeping you warm or
        A   B   C
    cool and protects the body from wear or tear.
                                    D

32. HGSE offers non-credit program, an intensive day program made of
                                      A   B
    combined skill courses plus a variety of electives.
            C   D

33. In addition to provide lodgings for strangers, the taverns of colonial
                    A   B
    America were also meeting places and centers of social life.
                        C   D

34. Sarah and Angelina Grimke <u>were among</u> the first women <u>lecturing in public</u>
                              A   B
in the United States.

總複習

I、請從以下四個選項中選出正確答案

1. By studying ancient pathologies, _____ to trace the development of diseases through the millenniums.
   (A) scientists hope
   (B) hopeful scientists
   (C) there is hope that scientists
   (D) they are hoping scientists can

2. No reptile or bird capable of detecting electric fields _____, but many kinds of fish and amphibians are equipped with electroreceptors.
   (A) been yet has found
   (B) has yet been found
   (C) found yet has been
   (D) found has been yet

3. Noah Webster, best known for his dictionary, _____also the first epidemiologist in the United States.
   (A) being
   (B) was
   (C) to be
   (D) having been

4. No machine can operate with total efficiency _____ friction of its parts consumes some of its energy.
   (A) with a
   (B) each of
   (C) because
   (D) why this

5. During the early period of ocean navigation, _____ any need for sophisticated instruments and techniques.

(A) so that hardly
(B) when there hardly was
(C) hardly was
(D) there was hardly

6. Lick Observatory is _____ observatory operated by the University of California.

(A) a mountaintop
(B) the top is a mountain
(C) the mountaintop has an
(D) the mountain on top

7. William Randolph Hearst, _____ eighteen newspapers and nine successful magazines, was one of the most flamboyant figures of the early twentieth century.

(A) he published them
(B) publisher of
(C) published by him
(D) that he was the publisher of

8. In 1647 the Massachusetts government passed a law _____, determining that education is a public responsibility.

(A) was a landmark
(B) that was a landmark
(C) is was a landmark that
(D) be a landmark

9. Not until 1984 did a major political party in the United States nominate a woman _____ its vice-presidential candidate.

(A) that is
(B) is to be
(C) to be
(D) being

10. On shallow ponds and canals of the Everglades in Florida, nutrient-fed algae _____ so thick that they block the sun from underwater plants.

(A) to grow   (B) growing

(C) it grows   (D) grow

11. The Impressionists tried to create paintings that captured a particular moment of _____, much as a camera does.

(A) reality is ever changing   (B) changing ever reality

(C) ever-changing reality   (D) changing reality ever

12. Often _____ of cured pork and beef, the frankfurter is one of the most popular sausages in the world.

(A) makes   (B) made

(C) to make   (D) is made

13. The species of life that exist on the shores of Cape Cod, _____ a short distance apart, are often quite diverse.

(A) they are only occasionally   (B) only occasionally are

(C) occasionally they only   (D) occasionally only

14. The characteristic of elasticity is _____ rubber from plastics and fibers.

(A) what they distinguish   (B) what distinguishes

(C) that distinguish   (D) distinguished

15. Billie Holiday is best known for the emotion _____ she brought to herinterpretations of popular songs.

(A) and   (B) why

(C) that   (D) how

II、請找出文法錯誤之處，且寫出正確答案

16. Agricultural technology has developed rapidly in the twentieth century
                              A   B   C

than in all previous history.
                 D

17. Pure tallow is white, tasteless, cream, and odorless.
    A   B   C   D

18. The Peakcock spreads its feathers into a gorgeous green and gold fan
                      A   B   C

when it courting the peahen.
             D

19. The Model-T Ford, a first popular, mass-produced car in the United
                      A   B

States, owed much of its success to Henry Ford's marketing strategies.
               C   D

20. Hazel Brannon Smith <u>she won</u> the Pulitzer Prize in 1964 for her
                         A
    editorials <u>supporting</u> the civil rights <u>movement</u>.
       B   C   D

21. <u>Metal</u> is an <u>efficient</u> conductor of electric current, but wood also
       A   B
    <u>permits</u> the <u>flew</u> of electrons to some extent.
       C   D

22. Because air is <u>denser</u> in cold weather, a wind of the same <u>speed</u> exerts
                      A   B
    25 percent <u>most</u> force during the winter <u>than</u> it does during the summer.
                  C   D

23. In the early eighteenth century, the violin <u>was using</u> <u>in</u> the orchestra
                                                    A   B
    <u>primarily</u> as an accompanying <u>instrument</u>.
        C   D

24. <u>Except for</u> Mercury and Venus, all the planets in <u>our</u> solar system <u>has</u>
        A   B   C
    one or <u>more</u> moons.
              D

25. An <u>organizer</u> of <u>the first</u> National Emigration Convention in 1854,
       A   B

   Martin Robinson Delany was an <u>officer army</u>, <u>physician</u>, and journalist.
                                  C   D

26. Sensations of <u>taste</u> have been determined <u>are</u> <u>strongly</u> interrelated <u>with</u>
            A   B   C   D

   sensations of smell.

27. Monkeys and apes are <u>extraordinarily communicative</u>, using <u>body language</u>
                           A   B

   and facial gestures to <u>tell the one another</u> <u>how they feel</u>.
                      C   D

28. Some people believe that the invention of the sewing needle <u>ranks</u> in
                                                A

   <u>important</u> with the invention of the wheel <u>and</u> the <u>discovery</u> of fire.
        B   C   D

29. The stars that <u>belong to</u> a group and move more or less <u>together</u> in
                A   B

   space <u>they all</u> have about <u>the same</u> space velocity.
          C   D

30. The distribution of <u>plants</u> <u>within</u> a region <u>are</u> directly related to <u>variations</u>
                     A   B   C   D

   in climate.

31. The Pennsylvania Company for Insurance <u>was</u> the first <u>commercial</u>
                                              A   B

    company in the United States <u>organized</u> <u>exclusive</u> for life insurance.
                                      C   D

32. It is <u>believed</u> that some dinosaurs <u>traveled</u> in herds, with the <u>young in</u>
            A   B   C

    the center and the adults on the sides <u>at</u> protection.
                                              D

33. The mythologies and <u>legends of</u> <u>ancient and modern</u> cultures possess
                            A   B

    an <u>enormously</u> spectrum of monsters and <u>imaginary</u> beasts.
          C   D

34. With <u>the</u> exception of Mandarin Chinese, the English <u>linguistics</u> is
            A   B

    <u>spoken</u> by more people than <u>any</u> other.
       C   D

35. The clear notes of the kettledrum are very finely <u>outline</u> and, as a
                                                          A

    result, kettledrummers <u>occasionally</u> have <u>solo</u> <u>passages</u> to play.
                                B   C   D

36. To Knit a scarf with hand, a person first places a row of loops on a
       A   B   C   D
   knitting needle.

37. Despite some of her verse is difficult to understand, Marianne Moore
       A   B
   crafted her poems superbly.
       C   D

38. Bette Davis became famous because her portrayals of strong-minded
                      A   B   C   D
   women in motion pictures.

39. Large quantity of lead in the atmosphere can have a damaging effect
            A   B   C
   on certain pollution-control mechanisms.
       D

40. Without the use of money, trade would be dependent on barter, the
                                      A
   direct exchange of one commodity from another.
       B   C   D

>>> Review 2

1. In The *Feminine Mystique*, Betty Friedan challenged _____ about the role of women in society.
   (A) long-established several attitudes
   (B) attitudes several long-established
   (C) several long-established attitudes
   (D) attitudes long-established several

2. Wars, famines, floods, and _____ have all caused migrations.
   (A) volcanoes erupt   (B) volcanic eruptions
   (C) with volcanoes erupting   (D) from volcanic eruptions

3. Numbers that can be expressed as the quotient of two integers _____ known as rational numbers.
   (A) is   (B) they are
   (C) are   (D) those are

4. A rheostat is resistor _____ regulates the flow of electrical current.
   (A) to   (B) one
   (C) there   (D) that

5. It is believed that the first astronomers observed the heavens _____ plan such seasonal activities as harvesting.
   (A) so   (B) thus
   (C) because of   (D) in order to

6. Hawaii produces more canned pineapple than _____ in the world.
   (A) other area (B) areas other than the
   (C) any other area (D) the other areas that

7. The first article of the United States Constitution gives Congress _____ _____ to pass laws.
   (A) the power (B) has the power
   (C) the power is (D) of the power

8. The brachiopods, _____, are commonly known as "lamp shells" because of their resemblance to Roman oil lamps.
   (A) a marine invertebrate phylum that
   (B) are a phylum of marine invertebrates which
   (C) a phylum of marine invertebrates which
   (D) a phylum of marine invertebrates

9. _____ than a fifth of the Earth's surface area is classified as permanent meadows and pastures.
   (A) There is less (B) It is less
   (C) Except for (D) Less

10. Using northern quahog clam shells, _____ that they strung together and used as money.
    (A) Native American beads were made
    (B) the making of beads of by Native Americans
    (C) Native Americans made beads
    (D) there were beads made by Native Americans

11. _____ one or more units of living substance called protoplasm.
   (A) All living things consist of
   (B) Although all living things that consist of
   (C) All living things consisting of
   (D) In all living things consisting of

12. A newspaper's political cartoons _____ capsule versions of editorial opinion.
   (A) serve as   (B) in serving
   (C) serves   (D) be served

13. Many, _____ animals with backbones have gallbladders.
   (A) they are not all   (B) but not all
   (C) not all, but   (D) but not all of

14. The photoperiodic response of algae actually depends on the duration of darkness, _____
   (A) the light is not on   (B) and not on light
   (C) but is not on the light (D) is not on light

15. _____ in the financial district of New York City, archaeologists have uncovered what they believe to be the remains of New York's first city hall.
   (A) Digs   (B) Digging
   (C) To be dug   (D) It is digging

II、請找出文法錯誤之處，且寫出正確答案

16. History sometimes effects a kind of reverse perspective in one's perception
    <u>A</u>   <u>B</u>

    of the past: events <u>appear</u> more significant the <u>far</u> away they get.
                               C   D

17. The First <u>modern</u> computer that successfully <u>use</u> vacuum tubes to do
                     A   B

    <u>mathematical</u> calculations <u>was constructed</u> in 1942 by John Atanasoff
          C   D

    and Clifford Berry.

18. <u>Through</u> the <u>study</u> of DNA, biochemistry <u>has</u> helped <u>explained</u> the
        A   B   C   D

    molecular basis of the laws of genetics.

19. <u>All of</u> the United States Presidents, James Buchanan is the <u>only one</u> <u>who</u>
      A   B   C

    was <u>not married</u>.
               D

20. <u>During the</u> War of 1812, British <u>ships</u> <u>stopped to</u> bringing <u>goods</u> to the
          A   B   C   D

    United States.

21. The name of Edwinton, North Dakota, was <u>changed</u> to Bismarck in
                                              A
    order <u>to attractive</u> German capital <u>to finance</u> to <u>construction</u> of the
          B   C   D
    Northern Pacific Railway.

22. A squid that has just been born <u>it will</u> follow <u>any</u> nearby moving
                                     A   B
    object <u>during</u> the <u>first few</u> days of its existence.
           C   D

23. <u>The</u> Statue of Liberty, a <u>huge</u> copper statue that <u>stands</u> in New York
    A   B   C
    Harbor, was <u>present</u> to the United States by France in 1884.
                D

24. Countries <u>grant</u> certain <u>rights</u> to their residents and <u>requires</u> certain
              A   B   C
    <u>duties</u> from them.
    D

25. Chemical engineering <u>deals with</u> the design, construction, and <u>operate</u>
                         A   B
    of plants and machinery <u>for</u> making <u>such products</u> as acids, dyes,
                            C   D
    drugs, and plastics.

26. A painter who lived most of his life in the Middle West, Grant Wood
　　 A　　　　　　　　　B　　　C

has called America's "Painter of the Soil."
　 D

27. Considered together, all bodies of water and ice make it up part of the
　　　　　　　　　　　　 A　　　　　　　　 B　　C　　 D

Earth called the hydrosphere.

28. The Liberty Bell is not longer rung regularly, but it has been rung on
　　　　　　　　　　 A　　　　　　　　　　　　　 B　　C

special occasions.
　　 D

29. When the late 1800's, many scientists in the United States were trying to
　　 A　　　　　　　　　　　　　　　　　　　　　　　　　　　　　 B

transmit speech electrically, but Alexander Graham Bell was the first
　　　　　　　　 C

to succeed.
　 D

30. Because humans have flexibility hands, creative brains, and the power
　　　 A　　　　　　　　　 B

of speech, they have come to dominate their environment.
　　　　　　　 C　　　　　　　　　　　　　　　 D

31. Chromosomes as appear long, tangled threads when they first become
               A   B   C

    visible during the early prophase stage of mitosis.
             D

32. Neon lights, like mercury and fluorescent, conduct electricity through
               A   B   C

    a gas give off light.
        D

33. Entertainer Sophie Tucker performed in a brassy, flamboyant style
                                             A

    that was equal effective for sentimental ballads and popular songs.
            B   C   D

34. Mountain ranges are important that they determine the climate and
                                A   B   C

    water flow of surrounding regions.
                     D

35. Carbon, as basic building block of all living cells, occurs in two stable
            A   B   C

    forms having atomic weights of 12 and 13, respectively.
        D

36. Many ancient legends <u>tell of</u> a great <u>prehistoric</u> flood that <u>severe</u>
                                  A   B   C
   reduced the world's <u>population</u>.
                    D

37. <u>In</u> years scientists have been <u>warning</u> that the ever-increasing
   A   B
   emissions of carbon dioxide <u>will warm</u> the globe with disastrous
                                C
   <u>consequences</u>.
      D

38. Phoebe Apperson Hearst <u>was noted</u> for her interest <u>in</u> talented people
                           A   B
   and her <u>serious</u> study <u>of</u> architect, music, and French.
            C   D

39. The <u>courage</u> and <u>heroic</u> of Kapiolani, high chief of Hawaii in the early
         A   B
   nineteenth century, <u>were</u> the <u>inspiration</u> for a poem by Tennyson.
                  C   D

40. <u>While ancient</u> times people simply painted inanimate objects, <u>during</u>
         A   B
   the Renaissance the painting <u>of</u> "still lifes" <u>developed</u> as an accepted
                              C   D
   art form.

問題解答

>>> **Exercise 1** 句子基本結構

1. A
2. C
3. A（run, ran, run, run by 運作）
4. B
5. C
6. C（The right...does not include the right... 或 The right is included in include the right.）
7. D（已有動詞 keeps，故 pass 改成分詞 passing）
8. B
9. D（with + 名詞片語）
10. C（of + 名詞片語）
11. C（主詞爲名詞片語）
12. B（from + 名詞片語）
13. C
14. B（主詞爲名詞片語）
15. D（主詞爲名詞片語，date back 追溯回去）
16. A, floor covering（樓板遮蔽物）
17. D, running through
18. B, 刪除 that
19. C, 刪除 and
20. B, is acknowledged（被承認，具法律效用）

>>> Exercise 2 名詞

1. B, simplicity（抽象名詞不用加 the）
2. A, Space（抽象名詞不用加 the）
3. C, air（空氣抽象名詞不可加 s）
4. A, editorial（社論）
5. C, on the basis（理論基礎）
6. B, computer literacy（電腦能力）
7. C, the maintenance
8. A, Long exposure（主詞是名詞片語）
9. C, the analysis
10. B, was（錢的總數視爲單數）
11. A, a
12. A, researchers（很多研究者）
13. B, is
14. C, to helping（to 是介系詞）
15. A, is
16. A, graduates
17. A, 9-story-high-rise（九層樓高）
18. C, shell beads（A number of 很多）
19. C, natural disasters（a series of Ns）
20. A, get（alumni 校友們）
21. A, the number of（可投票人數增加）
22. B, a number of
23. C, individuals
24. C, a hundred blend of（a blend of 一個組合）
25. A, blood vessels（兩個名詞再一起，前者爲形容詞）
26. B, of（組成，three part copper 三分的銅）
27. C, student population（兩個名詞再一起，前者爲形容詞）
28. B, blood cells（兩個名詞再一起，前者爲形容詞）

29. C, the Nile

30. C, the Mediterranean Sea

31. D, every four years

32. A, Large amounts of

33. B, that cross（curricula 是複數）

34. B, an ethic

35. A, has（一本書是單數）

36. C, by means of

37. B（原句 It is estimated 150 of the 500 languages that were once spoken by the Chinese exist today. 為了強調只有 150 語言存在今天，把形容詞子句前提。It is estimated 經常簡寫成 an estimated）

38. D, its（指 body's）

39. A, it（指 bite）

40. C, those（指 clocks）

41. C, them（指 other metals）

42. C, our

43. C, their scholarly（指 members）

44. C, themselves（指 Negroes）

45. B, which is（錢總數視為單數）

46. C, the others（其餘全部的物種）

47. D, country（any other + 單數名詞）

48. D, one another

49. B, commodity（any other + 單數名詞）

50. C, those（指 rights）

51. D, other

52. C, other

53. A, another

54. C, by means of

55. D, to each（對兩者皆是 common to each）

>>> **Exercise 3 動詞 I**

1. D（witness（及物動詞）見證…的發生地點／時間 The decade...witnessed a continued emphasis 教育上一個持續強調發生在 1960s 年代）

2. A, enabling（已有動詞 must be，避免雙動詞，enable 改成分詞修飾主詞）

3. C, has come（完成式 come, came, come）

4. B, be inaugurated

5. C, are owned by（owe to 欠…債）

6. D, led to（lead, led, led）

7. A, to regard thoughts（decide to, decision to V）

8. B, were left（leave, left, left）

9. C, keeps（主詞 a ray of light 單數）

10. B, has gained

11. B, be fitted neatly

12. A, include（一般事實，用現在式即可；third parties 第三方可以是不只一個對象）

13. D, are collectively terms（主詞是 ways）

14. D, deepens（兩個動詞做平行架構，deep 是形容詞）

15. B, required to meet

16. C, was made（1973 是過去事件）

17. A, allow（一般事實，用現在式即可）

18. C, in quality（原句爲 which differs from ordinary light considerably in quality）

19. A, which sets（which 是指 a country 爲單數）

20. C, comes from（一般事實，用現在式即可）

21. B, reflect（一般事實，用現在式即可）

22. D, to transmit（be able/ the ability to V）

23. D, for（或 since ten years ago）

24. D, the year before（數＋ago, 如 3 years ago）

25. C, have increased（Over... 用完成式）

26. B, transmitting

27. D, to customers' satisfactions（commitment to 介系詞非不定詞）

28. A, to helping（dedicate to 介系詞非不定詞）

29. B, Consuming（動名詞當主詞）

30. C, knowing（或 the knowledge of）

31. C, in recognizing（difficulty/ trouble in）

32. B, working（spend＋V-ing）

33. B. are taken（take steps 採取步驟）

34. C, do（do harm 造成傷害）

35. C, has taken place（since 採完成式）

36. A, are（一般事實，用現在式即可）

37. C, has（主詞 vaporization 是單數）

38. A, do（do their best）

39. B, do（do research）

40. B, made（make debut 首次出現在公眾）

41. B, to correct（The aim is to V）

42. B, to increase（目的）

43. B, is referred to as（意指）

44. A, have been placed on/ upon（著重於）

45. C, been offered（去 to, be offered a second nomination 被提供連任提名）

46. D, have（fish 單複數同形）

47. C, exist（there 是虛主詞，真正主詞是 nationalism and racism）

48. D（...was considered the greatest educator by most Chinese...）

49. C（...is regarded the most theoretical physicist since Einstein by scientists）

>>> Exercise 4 動詞 II

1. D, split（split, split, split; suggests that...+（should）原形動詞，所以 have 沒錯）

2. B, be（should be, should 被省略）

3. C, have（should have, should 被省略）

4. B, be entitled（should be entitled to 與生具有權利，should 被省略）

5. D, be outlawed（should be outlawed, should 被省略）

6. C, have（should have, should 被省略））

7. D, stay（should find a job and stay out of trouble, should 被省略）

8. D, severe enough（enough 為副詞，置修飾語之後）

9. D（If 子句為可能未來，採簡單現在式）

10. D（If 子句為不可能未來或不希望發生之未來，採 were to V）

11. B（If 子句與過去事實相反，採過去簡單式，原句為 If there had been no improvements, 省略 If, had 倒裝到句首）

12. B（原句為 If the ice...were to melt, 省略 If, were 倒裝到句首，代表和未來事實相反，因此主句採 would +V）

13. A（原句為 The fact that the Earth revolved around the sun...if Galileo had not cared...，if 被省略，所以 had 倒裝，代表與過去事實相反，所以主句採 would have not V-en）如果 Galileo 不是很執著且很喜歡證明當時人們信仰的錯誤和荒繆，地球繞著態氧轉的事實就不會被發現。

14. A（The flowers would have grown well 花應該長得很好的，是與過去事實相反的假設句子，but 後則接一個過去的事實，but Eva 老是忘了澆水）

15. C, would have been（和過去事實相反）

16. C, might not have rebelled（和過去事實相反）

17. B, had fallen through（和過去事實相反）

18. D, did not occur（和現在事實相反）

19. A, were（和現在事實相反，你要是多關心我一點就好）

20. D, happened（和現在事實相反）
21. C, had it not been（和過去事實相反，原句為 if it had not been due to，省略 if）
22. A, would（和現在事實相反）
23. A, were（和現在事實相反）
24. D, are given（unless 之後是事實，不是假設句）
25. A, would have been（和過去事實相反）
26. C, causing（melted 是動詞，在沒有連接詞的時候，caused 需轉換成分詞作修飾 glaciers）
27. C, seeking to
28. B, well-arranged hues（well-arranged 做形容詞）
29. B, extracted from（修飾 oil）
30. B, regarded
31. C, has furthered（進一步，深入）
32. C, be made of（組成）
33. C, check
34. B, vary（採動詞）
35. B, portraying

>>> Exercise 5 形容詞與副詞

1. B（致命的）
2. D（一個平衡的飲食）
3. D（主要地）
4. D（貧窮侵襲的家庭）
5. A, highly corrosive（修飾形容詞採複詞）
6. D, long-haired
7. D, power-driven（動力驅動的）
8. A, thimble-shaped（造型的）
9. B, wool-producing
10. C, particularly,
11. D, wide/ in width
12. C, lengths
13. D, none
14. D, somewhat
15. C, it really is
16. A, richly-colored
17. D, orderly and equable
18. B, mostly
19. C, safely
20. A currently
21. D, equal
22. C, intensely-animated
23. C, animal（animal and vegetable origins）
24. A, most
25. C, sufficient enough
26. A, usually considered
27. D, nearby
28. A, web-footed

29. A, incomparable
30. D, covered
31. A, typically
32. B, alone（獨居）
33. C, hurriedly（years-long 數年來的，year-long 一整年的）
34. B, uniquely
35. A, nearly
36. B, almost（幾乎）
37. A, Unlike
38. B, most
39. A, observed directly
40. C, readily

>>> Exercise 6 There, It

1. D（這句子需要主動詞）
2. B
3. B（There are several different methods (that) people use（形容詞子句）to...
4. C
5. A（an estimated one million American women 根據估計有一百萬美國女性…）
6. B
7. A
8. A
9. B
10. C（there is evidence 或 it is evident，很明顯地）
11. D
12. B
13. D
14. B, that the university
15. C, are

>>> **Exercise 7 合句**

1. D
2. D
3. D
4. C
5. C
6. D
7. D
8. C（with + 名詞片語，三個形容詞修飾一個名詞 designs）
9. A（is + 3 個平行的形容詞；介系詞 + 名詞做修飾語）
10. B（not only + 子句（倒裝句），but also + 子句）
11. C, of mutual needs
12. D, offer
13. B because of the desirable location
14. D, had
15. D, beauty（as well as 兩邊要成平行架構）
16. D, C, clearness
17. C, but
18. D, neither
19. B, buries
20. D, coated with
21. B, serious（serious 和 irreversible damage）
22. C, free inquiry
23. D, teach them
24. B, because
25. D, its location
26. A, Both
27. D, industrial
28. C, wealthy
29. B, soft metal
30. A, do artificial reefs（Not only + 倒裝句）

>>> **Exercise 8** 副詞子句

1. C（Although + 子句，主詞 + 動詞）
2. C（分詞構句修飾主句的主詞 western chemists）
3. B（guided 修飾主句的主詞 scientists）
4. A（influenced 修飾主句的主詞 Martin）
5. D（兩子句需要一個副詞連接詞 whereas 然而，in that 因為，thus 是副詞）
6. C（兩個矛盾的子句需要一個副詞連接詞 but）
7. A（enforced 修飾主句的主詞 the existing law）
8. B（原句 before they received a visa, they 省略，動詞 received 改成分詞 receiving）
9. D（副詞子句要有連接詞，as winter approaches 隨著冬天來臨）
10. A（是 if magnesium is properly combined 的省略）
11. D（兩子句需要一個副詞連接詞 although）
12. A（Despite 儘管，為介系詞 + 名詞片語）
13. C（compared 修飾主句的主詞 a tornado）
14. C（兩子句需要一個副詞連接詞 unless 除非）
15. D（With + 名詞片語，隨著）
16. D（With + 名詞片語，隨著）
17. C（Instead of + 名詞片語，…替代、不做）
18. B.
19. D（unlike 介系詞，不像，dislike 動詞，不喜歡）
20. B
21. A（as 連接詞，因為）
22. B（when it is seasoned, it 之省略句）
23. A（for 連接詞）
24. C（除了產生心理上的回饋之外，放輕鬆能… ）
25. B（直到最近）
26. B（It was...that 分裂句）

27. C（not until 的主句要倒裝）

28. B（Until 直到）

29. D（Until 直到）

30. A（Wherever 連接詞，無論到哪旅行）

31. B（原句 Merino sheep were originally bred，之省略主詞、be 動詞）

32. B（no matter how 形容詞／副詞＋子句）

33. D（wherever 無論何處）

34. A（Despite）

35. A（Thanks to　由於）

36. B（because of）

37. A（Founded 創立）

38. C（刪除 but）

39. C（thereby 是副詞，故動詞 proved 要改成分詞 proving）

40. A（Because of）

>>> **Exercise 9 形容詞子句**

1. D
2. C（which 修飾 stars）
3. B
4. C（each of which 指 each of two parts 之轉換）
5. C（who 修飾 those）
6. A（on which 修飾 stalks）
7. D（from which 即 from the college education）
8. D
9. B（by which 即 by the world standard）
10. D
11. B（where the winds= wherever the winds）
12. A（to which = to the surfaces）
13. D
14. D（where 指 registration office）
15. B（which 指 massive glaciers melted 這件事）
16. D（原句 each has genes... 因沒有連接詞，故 has 改成 with）
17. B（a number of which 指 a number of woods）
18. A（which 指 a transfer of power）
19. D
20. A
21. B（原句 ...people...can get the protein that their bodies required from the food that they eat. 兩個 that 代受詞，可省略）
22. D（including + 名詞）
23. B
24. B（where 指 forums 專欄）
25. C（where 指 base 基地）
26. A（原句 ...they（指 financial program）are intended to encourage students of colors to...，故使用 whom 代之）

27. D（...poisonous claws, which, located behind the head, are dangerous. located behind the head 修飾 claws）

28. A（教育是科學因為（in that）教育學者使用一組嚴格的科學方法⋯）

29. D（原句 ... substance which is known to science. which is 省略）

30. B（名詞片語 the preservation of ... 作 individualism 同位語）

31. B（during which 指 during photosynthesis 光合作用）

32. B（whose inspiration 指 Chaplin 帶來的激勵）

33. C（改成 who 指 people in Ethiopia）

34. B（... all the water (that) they need 中 that 省略）

35. B（in which 指 environment）

36. B（刪掉 it）

37. A（who drop 主詞是 students 複數）

38. B（faculty 是教師們，故連接代名詞用 who are）

39. C（刪除 is）

40. A（刪除 by, which 指 custom）

Exercise 10 名詞子句

1. A（reported 連接兩個名詞子句 that the gap ... and that 主詞（what lies ahead...）+ is a region of...）
2. B（The fact (that the...world) 主詞 + has improved）
3. C（(That the child... 主詞) was a miracle. 奇蹟是事實或事件）
4. D（It is proved that 證實的是一件事實）
5. B（for 後面只銜接名詞或 w-/h- 名詞子句）
6. A（What the scientists fear 科學家所害怕的是甚麼，為主詞 + is）
7. C（about 後面只銜接名詞或 w-/h- 名詞子句）
8. D（are + 名詞子句做補語，能代主詞的名詞連接詞為 what）
9. C（that 子句作為 the theory 的同位語）
10. C（兩個選項的名詞子句連接詞為 whether...or）
11. D（to 為介系詞後面只銜接名詞／名詞子句，what 代受詞）
12. B（verify/prove/imply + that 名詞子句）
13. D（verify/prove/imply + that 名詞子句）
14. A（find + that 名詞子句）
15. B（of 後面只銜接名詞／名詞子句，what 代主詞）
16. B（of 後面只銜接名詞／名詞子句，what 代主詞）
17. A（of 後面只銜接名詞／名詞子句，what 代受詞）
18. D（of 後面只銜接名詞／名詞子句，what 代主詞）
19. D（of 後面只銜接名詞／名詞子句，what 代主詞）
20. B
21. D（of 後面只銜接名詞／名詞子句）
22. C（of 後面只銜接名詞／名詞子句，what 代主詞）
23. B（that all... 名詞子句作為 view 的同位語）
24. D（It is ..that）
25. A（a chemical reaction 作為 fermentation 發酵的同位語）
26. D（Fermium 作為 a metallic element 的同位語）
27. C（主句需要動詞）

28. A（the oldest institution 作爲 Harvard University 的同位語）

29. C（主句，需要主、動詞）

30. C（Alexander 作爲 bacteriologist 的同位語）

31. C（the same year 作爲 1770 的同位語）

32. B（a pragmatist 作爲 Dewey 的同位語）

33. B（主句：主詞＋動詞）

34. A（同位語）

35. C, what（destroy ＋ 名詞子句，what 代子句主詞）

36. B, whether（over ＋ wh- 子句，選項的連接詞爲 whether）

37. A, is that values（that values... 名詞子句作爲 intelligence 補語）

38. A, in what（There is a great gap in ＋ 名詞子句）

39. A, When（青銅何時首次使用在亞洲）

40. A, What would be（凡是在戲劇中相當長的演說是用敍唱的方式呈現）

>>> Exercise 11 比較結構

1. C（The more, the less 的句型）
2. D（The coarser the sediment (is), the less...(is) 的句型，省略 is）
3. D（the adj-er + the 名詞片語）
4. D（原句 the greater the amount of paper (which is) used，省略）
5. A（The more, the more awesome 的句型）
6. D（The more, the easier 的句型）
7. D（原句 the more the opportunity (which are) offered，which are 省略）
8. A（it 需主詞代替 to speed it up or slow it down）
9. D（that runs off 修飾 precipitation）
10. A（原句 The damage...grows worse when the exposure to... increased more 主句不改變，而子句的 the more 提到子句的句首，when 則省略）
11. A（原句 A body weighs less when it gets farther from the surface of the Earth. 主句不改變，而子句的 the farther 提到子句的句首，when 則省略）
12. A（相同詞性才能比較，that 是 the annual worth 之代名詞）
13. A（相同詞性才能比較，that 是 judicial system 之代名詞，does 倒裝到子句的句首）
14. C（相同詞性才能比較，those 是 proposals 之代名詞，do 倒裝到子句的句首）
15. B（相同詞性才能比較，the ratio of managers' salaries to those of ordinary workers）
16. A（than + 子句）
17. A（原句 Eastern Taiwan receives...than Western Taiwan does. 倒裝 does 到子句的句首）
18. B（不是）
19. B（as much by frustration as by success 平行句構）

20. B, faster

21. C, as

22. C, as（as little chance of accident as possible）

23. C, is more

24. C, that（指 energy）

25. D, adults'（和 children's memory 做比較）

26. C, much more（much more susceptible than...）

27. D, the lighter

28. B, higher education（高等教育）

29. C, far more common（far + 比較及形容詞）

30. B, far greater（far + 比較及形容詞）

31. C, later（後來，latter 後者）

32. D, actually are.

33. C, Ireland's（兩個地方的人口比較）

34. D, most unusual（Among... 做最高級的比較）

35. D, than were（對稱比較 be V）

36. C, that（對稱 goods worth 貨物價值）

37. C, twice as much meat...as

38. C, than（less...than）

39. A, the unique（unique 獨一無二，沒有比較級變化）

40. B, most distinctive

>>> **Exercise 12 倒裝句**

1. B（Not until 主句要倒裝）
2. B（By no means 否定意義，主句要倒裝）
3. C（Only when 主句要倒裝）
4. C（Not until 主句才需要倒裝）
5. A
6. D（原句 The force exerted by typhoons is so great that it has...，So great 倒裝到句首強調力度很大）
7. B（原句 Lillian Hellman was so successful...that...，So successful 倒裝到句首）
8. B, have（Only 主句要倒裝）
9. C, nor are
10. B, is（主句的主詞是 the world; largest forest 單數，故倒裝的動詞為 is）
11. C, as well as
12. A, Such is（原句的主句動詞為 is）
13. C, can we（only by accepting... 主句要倒裝）

>>> Exercise 13 介系詞

1. A, Prior to 1914
2. C, upon
3. B, till
4. A, In
5. A, native to（原生種）
6. C, at
7. C, responsible for
8. A, Unlike
9. A, comes from
10. D, upon
11. D, for
12. D, in huge flocks
13. C, by far
14. D, in（result in 導致）
15. D, to
16. B, similar to
17. D, at
18. C, remind us of
19. D, at
20. D, on credit（in cash）
21. C, with
22. C, according to
23. D, from fakes（distinguish A from B）
24. B, from
25. B, upon
26. A, to improving
27. B, composed of
28. C, on

29. C, to（subject to 受制於）

30. A, with

31. C, in

32. B, made up of（組成）

33. A, to providing

34. B, to lecture（the first...to V）

>>> 總複習 Review 1

1. A（簡單句架構）
2. B（主句，完成式）
3. B（簡單句架構）
4. C（因果關係副詞子句）
5. D（簡單句架構）
6. A（名詞片語）
7. B（同位語）
8. B（形容詞子句）
9. C（成為）
10. D（主句動詞）
11. D（of + 名詞片語）
12. B（分詞構句）
13. D（同位語）
14. B（what 子句作為主詞補語，what 代子句主詞）
15. C（形容詞子句 that 即 emotion）
16. B, developed more rapidly
17. C, creamy
18. D, courts
19. A, the
20. B. editorials（社論）
21. D, flow
22. C, more
23. A, used
24. C, have
25. C, army officer
26. B, 刪除 are
27. C, tell one another
28. B, importance

29. C, 刪除 they
30. C, is
31. D, exclusively
32. D, for
33. C, enormous
34. B, language
35. A, outlined
36. B, with hands
37. A, Although
38. B, because of
39. A, qualities
40. D, with

>>> 總複習 Review 2

1. C（名詞片語為 challenge 受詞）
2. B（平行句構）
3. C（主動詞）
4. D（形容詞子句）
5. D
6. C
7. A
8. D（同位語）
9. D
10. C
11. A
12. A
13. D
14. B（光合作用依賴…而不是依賴…）
15. B（分詞構句，digging 修飾 archaeologists）
16. D, farther（原句 ..., events appear more significant when they get farther away. 雙重比較，主句不改變，子句的比較形容詞提到子句句首，省略 when）
17. B, using
18. C, explain
19. A, Among all of
20. C, 刪除 to
21. B, to attract
22. A, 刪除 it
23. D, presented
24. C, require
25. B, operation
26. D, was called

27. C, 刪除 it
28. A, no longer
29. A, In
30. B, flexible hands
31. A, appear as
32. D, and give off
33. B, equally
34. A, in that（因爲）
35. A, as a basic
36. C, severely（tell of 述說）
37. A, for
38. D, architecture
39. B, heroism
40. A, During

國家圖書館出版品預行編目資料

英語文法與修辭／陳錦芬著. -- 初版.
-- 臺北市：五南圖書出版股份有限公司,
2020.12
面； 公分
ISBN 978-986-522-392-2（平裝）

1.英語 2.語法

805.16   109020627

1XJU

英語文法與修辭

作　　者 ― 陳錦芬（253.7）

發 行 人 ― 楊榮川

總 經 理 ― 楊士清

總 編 輯 ― 楊秀麗

副總編輯 ― 黃文瓊

責任編輯 ― 吳雨潔

封面設計 ― 姚孝慈

美術設計 ― 姚孝慈

出 版 者 ― 五南圖書出版股份有限公司

地　　址：106台北市大安區和平東路二段339號4樓

電　　話：(02)2705-5066　　傳　　真：(02)2706-6100

網　　址：https://www.wunan.com.tw

電子郵件：wunan@wunan.com.tw

劃撥帳號：01068953

戶　　名：五南圖書出版股份有限公司

法律顧問　林勝安律師

出版日期　2020年12月初版一刷
　　　　　2024年 3 月初版二刷

定　　價　新臺幣300元

經典永恆・名著常在

五十週年的獻禮——經典名著文庫

五南，五十年了，半個世紀，人生旅程的一大半，走過來了。

思索著，邁向百年的未來歷程，能為知識界、文化學術界作些什麼？

在速食文化的生態下，有什麼值得讓人雋永品味的？

歷代經典・當今名著，經過時間的洗禮，千錘百鍊，流傳至今，光芒耀人；

不僅使我們能領悟前人的智慧，同時也增深加廣我們思考的深度與視野。

我們決心投入巨資，有計畫的系統梳選，成立「經典名著文庫」，

希望收入古今中外思想性的、充滿睿智與獨見的經典、名著。

這是一項理想性的、永續性的巨大出版工程。

不在意讀者的眾寡，只考慮它的學術價值，力求完整展現先哲思想的軌跡；

為知識界開啟一片智慧之窗，營造一座百花綻放的世界文明公園，

任君遨遊、取菁吸蜜、嘉惠學子！